Giving Chase

by

JoMarie DeGioia

Giving Chase

Book Eight of the
Cypress Corners Series

by

JoMarie DeGioia

Chapter 1

Cypress Corners, Florida

"You don't have to do that, man."

Chase Harris looked over at his cousin Billy as they waited for their drinks at the coffee shop.

"Yeah, I do." He shoved his hands in his pockets. "Besides, it's literally the least I can do."

Billy smiled, looking a lot like the orphan he'd been when Chase's father had taken him in all those years ago. "Thanks, man."

Billy might be his cousin, but he'd been raised as a brother even though they were never close growing up. Chase shouldered the blame for that, he and his dick of a brother Zach. Neither of them had made a place for Billy, and when his father had left a fortune to him? Chase had been a little pissed and let Billy know it. That was only one of the things he'd been trying to atone for where his cousin was concerned.

Wild Harry Harris hadn't shown any more affection towards Billy than he had to Chase and Zach. That didn't stop Chase from missing his father though, dead and gone since last summer. In truth, he didn't begrudge Billy his inheritance since he and Zach shared the ranch over in St. Cloud. His father had known cattle, and he and Zach had learned enough to turn the ranch into a moneymaker.

He and Billy got their drinks and headed out into the February sunshine. There was a slight chill in the air, and Chase took in a deep breath. The air here in Cypress, a sprawling property of ten thousand acres featuring upscale retail, state-of-the-art homes and an award-winning golf course, was surprisingly fresh. And since his brother was making noise about buying Chase out of his share of the ranch, he figured it might be a decent place to settle. Billy sure had found his own home here.

They sat down at a table beneath a winter-bare tree hung with paper hearts. The damn things seemed to be everywhere. It was like Valentine's Day threw up all over the town square.

"So why isn't Shannon going with you to Serenity Shores?" Chase asked as he took the lid off of his cup.

Billy chuckled. "You know, I had to do some pretty fast talking to get her to leave the Crescent Resort, but now I can't drag her away from Cypress."

Billy's new wife was a beauty and a great girl, from what Chase could tell. Billy had met her in St. Cloud, but had gone down to Serenity Shores on the gulf to bring her back. From where Chase was sitting, it had been a good move for him.

"You got her wedded and bedded, Billy. Nice job."

Billy smiled again. Chase's chest tightened. This guy was friendly and easygoing, and could have been a great friend growing up. They were the same age, twenty-nine, and should have been close. They were both tall, broad and dark-haired, and looked a lot alike except for the eyes. Billy's were blue but Chase had hazel eyes like his mother.

They had both been ten years old when Billy's parents were killed in a car crash. Maybe if Chase's mother had been around things might have been different, but she'd taken off with an equipment salesman two years before Billy had moved in.

"Tell me what you need," he told Billy.

"You've been a big help out at the worksite, Chase."

Chase nodded. "Yeah."

"The plans are coming along, thanks to the work of the Cypress architect."

"He's supposed to be the best," Chase said.

"It's no big deal if I don't go down to Serenity Shores right away."

Chase leveled a look at him. "This woman, this Jo Potter?" At Billy's nod he went on. "She has some samples and other some such for you, right?"

"Yeah."

"Something she can't mail?"

Billy smiled and wiped a hand over his jaw. "No. She doesn't want to mail it."

Chase spread his hands. "Then leave it to me. I'll go get whatever it is and bring it back to you."

Billy tilted his head. "Why?"

Chase blew out a breath. "Because you're family."

"Like that ever mattered to you."

Chase nodded. "I know. I was a prick. I aim to fix that, if you'll let me."

"You know I'm a big believer in second chances, Chase."

Yeah, he was. His life was built on them, and now he had a perfect woman to share it with.

Chase thought for a second about Carrie, the spunky red-haired friend of the bride who Chase got to know biblically at Billy and Shannon's wedding. He'd still been stinging from his ex-wife Cheyanne's swift exit six months before. Carrie had been sweet and hot and just what he'd needed to forget the implosion of his dismal, short-lived marriage.

"So give me whatever I need and I'll head out tomorrow," Chase said.

Billy turned his coffee cup on the table. "I booked a one-week stay at the resort."

"A whole week?" Chase gaped at him. "Why?"

A smile teased his cousin's mouth. "Nostalgia, I guess."

Chase gave a slow nod. "That was where you won back your girl."

"Yep. The Crescent Resort is amazing. The view of the gulf, the tropical setting of Crescent Key. I think you could use a break. Why not stay there and chill for a week?"

Chase sat back and crossed his arms. "I couldn't do that."

"Why not? Didn't you say Zach wants to handle the ranch from now on?"

Irritation bit at Chase's belly. "Yeah, he does. Wants to run the place like a damn business."

"It is a business."

"Don't you start."

Billy held up his hands. "Hey, I don't have a stake in the ranch. I just think you can do with a little bit of an escape."

Chase wondered just how much Billy knew about Chase's failed marriage. He'd downed a lot of liquor at the wedding, and he remembered bitching and moaning about his ex to just about anybody who would listen. He didn't normally drink that much, but being in the sight of such a love like Billy and Shannon had? It had been the last straw.

A paper heart broke free above him and fluttered down to land in his coffee. Muttering a curse, he fished it out and slapped it down on the table. "What the hell is with all the hearts?"

"It's almost Valentine's Day, cuz," Billy said.

"So? Cypress has been dressed like a two-dollar whore for weeks now."

Billy laughed and Chase found a smile. "Go down to Serenity Shores, man. Maybe you can look up a certain friend of Shannon's while you're there."

Chase thought again about Carrie. They'd had a real good time out at that secluded tent-cabin thing on the far lakeshore. The memories were clear despite all the drinking he'd done, and gave a whole new meaning to the words "great outdoors." No words were ever exchanged that their encounter was anything more than two people scratching an itch, though.

"We kind of put a period on the end of that sentence, Billy."

"Maybe you can show her that a period isn't necessarily the only end to a sentence."

Chase felt a smile curve his lips. "Maybe."

***

Crescent Resort & Spa
Serenity Shores, Crescent Key, Florida

"A period is just the end of a sentence," Carrie Boyles murmured as she stacked the creamy goats-milk soaps on their display.

The tall round table was draped with a sheer yet rustic length of net fabric in a soft rose, the color picking up the pink tones in the bars of soap set on top. These were some of Jo Potter's best, handmade and so popular Carrie felt like she spent half of her time restocking. Giving a nod, she tweaked the raffia bows dressing the soaps.

Valentine's Day had made its way in here too, from the decorated lobby of the resort. Pretty, pierced-paper hearts dripped from the ceiling and the shop carried more items intended for use by couples than they normally did. Just a couple of months ago she would have grabbed up all of the luscious-looking soaps and washes to share with Doug. Ugh, not now.

Stepping back, she pulled off her lacy headband and brushed her hair back from her face before setting it back on her head. A period might be the end of a sentence, but oh what she wouldn't give to see one right now. It would be way more welcome than the little blue lines she'd seen this morning on that plastic stick. It was nearly three-thirty on a Wednesday afternoon, hours had passed, and she still couldn't shake her shock. How the heck had this happened?

She'd worked in the shop at Crescent for nearly a year now, and the small retail space adjacent to the Serenity Spa felt like home to her. The fact that she had the absolute best boss in the world in Marion Tucker might have something to do with it. That, and the New Age music tinkling softly over the sound system the shop shared with the spa next door.

She ran her hands over her uniform, consisting of a crisp white wraparound shirt topping khaki capris. It might be February, but the weather on the gulf was pretty mild most days. Come the evenings it might drop into the mid-fifties, so she often needed the cardigan she brought with her for after her day's work was done. Right now, though? Her clothes, the shop, her present-tense felt very insular. Safe.

On her feet she wore a pair of her ballet flats, in pink leather today. They were super soft and resilient. Resilient. Just like she hoped to be. These shoes were staying on her feet, too. No more of that "toes in the sand, heart in your hand" stuff Serenity Shores was famous for. Been there, done that, got the T-shirt.

"What's with that look, Carrie?" her boss asked from beneath the archway separating the two spaces.

Carrie shook her head with a smile. "What look?"

Marion smirked at her. "You're glaring at your shoes. Pinching, are they?"

"No. Not at all." Carrie took a breath and straightened her shoulders. "They're very comfortable. I might never take them off."

The other woman's eyes sparkled and Carrie knew she'd gotten her message loud and clear.

"And here I thought after you got back from Cypress Corners last month that you might be open to falling in love again."

Carrie stilled. Cypress Corners. That little slice of almost-wilderness in Central Florida where she'd gone for her friend Shannon's wedding last month. Where she'd hooked up with a hot guy saddled with more baggage than even she'd dragged up there. A hot guy she hadn't been able to stop thinking about since, but still. And where, apparently, she'd acquired the little tagalong she'd never expected.

"Nope." Carrie shook her head. "Never again."

Marion came closer. "Because of that ass hat?"

"Doug plays a big part in my decision, yes. The fact that he cheated right here at Crescent? Yeah, that sucked." She blew out a breath. "It's more than that, though. I'm done with the whole thing."

Marion laughed, tossing her long dark hair over one shoulder. "Honey, you're way too young to be so bitter."

Carrie found a smile. "I'm twenty-seven, I'll have you know."

Marion snorted. "A baby. That's what you are." She placed her hands on Carrie's shoulder. "Didn't you have a ringside seat for Shannon's fall last summer?"

"Yes, and she and Billy Goat are ridiculously happy now."

"*Theirs* was a second chance."

Carrie shook her head again. "They were in love, Marion. Truly in love. It was clear whenever you saw the two of them together."

"And you weren't?"

Carrie bit her lip. "I thought I was. Doug clearly didn't feel the same way, despite the fact that he told me he did so many times I'd lost count."

"So you're going to let that slug dictate the course of the rest of your life?"

14

Carrie paused for a beat. "That's the big question, isn't it?"

Marion stepped back. "You don't have to make a decision today on the rest of your life, although Valentine's Day is just around the corner. You, my dear, have all the time in the world."

Carrie lips thinned but she just nodded again. All the time in the world? Not if that stinkin' plastic stick was right.

Thankfully the whoosh of the doors to the spa opening reached them through the archway. Marion patted her arm and breezed back into the spa.

Shannon had worked the front desk last summer, until her Billy Goat had come and swept her off her sandy toes. Now Carrie's boss was trying out a rotation of semi-competent people to fill Shannon's shoes. Carrie had no horse in that race, though. Her job was to sell the amazing products that the spa massage therapists and receptionists, hopefully, recommended. These soaps? They were the most popular item the spa shop carried.

Crossing her arms, she took in a breath. She was pregnant. From her one fling that never should have been flung in the first place. Oh, but Chase Harris was so hot. His smile had been a surprise, since it had been his brooding expression that had first caught her eye at Shannon and Billy's reception. He was Billy's cousin, and the two men were nearly a matched pair. Tall dark and

15

handsome with twinkling eyes and dimples. Chase had looked a little dangerous, though. Like he'd needed something more than the bottle of beer he'd been nursing. Like he'd needed her.

"There's someone looking for you, Carrie," a white-blond spiky-haired young woman said from the archway.

Carrie looked over at Spiky-hair. This was the fourth receptionist this week, and Carrie had given up on learning their names until at least one of them stuck.

"Me?" she asked.

"Yeah," a man's voice said from behind Spiky-hair.

Carrie knew that voice. Oh, it was deep and a little rumbly and the last time she'd heard it was when the man attached to the voice had murmured the sweetest and naughtiest things in her ear. Things she'd played over and over in her dreams since.

Chase Harris stepped into the shop, his hazel eyes locked on her and a smile just teasing those sculpted lips. Darn it, he looked as good as she'd remembered.

"Hey, Red."

And with those two words, that silly nickname she should hate but secretly loved, Carrie's safe and insular world cracked wide open.

Crap.

Chapter 2

Chase watched as Carrie's cheeks went a little white. Maybe he hadn't called her since the night of Billy's wedding. Yeah, he could be a prick that way. His ex-wife had made that perfectly clear. Since the divorce last fall he'd kept to himself. Carrie was the first woman he'd gotten remotely close to. Physically, anyway. He hadn't expected her to look so shocked to see him, though.

"Hi, there." He stepped closer to Carrie as the spa's receptionist turned and went back to her desk. "How've you been?"

"Hi, Chase." Carrie visibly swallowed. "I'm good. You?"

He shrugged in answer. "Good. I'm here for Billy."

She blinked those long lashes he'd noticed from the first, her pretty blue eyes wide. "He's not here."

He smiled and rubbed a hand over his jaw. "Yeah. I mean I'm here on his behalf."

She fiddled with the ties on the bars of soap like the ones he'd seen at Billy's place. Goats-milk soap that Billy and Shannon hoped to recreate at their farm in Cypress.

"So…you're here to visit the Potter's farm?"

Chase nodded. "Yes. Jo Potter has some things she needs me to take back to Cypress."

"Why didn't Billy come down?" Carrie clasped her hands, her eyes bright now. "I would have loved to see Shannon again."

Chase grinned as he thought about the conversation with his cousin yesterday. "Billy said he can't drag her out of Cypress now."

"She did look ridiculously happy at the wedding."

"That's the thing about weddings, Red." His lips thinned. "Everybody looks happy at weddings."

Clouds seem to gather over her face. "I guess that's true."

"It sure was at mine." He winced. "Damn, sorry. I'm not supposed to dwell on that, or so Shannon says."

"She *is* the queen of second chances, you know."

Chase saw the sparkle in Carrie's eye. Once again that rush he'd felt at the wedding went through him. She was both hot and adorable, and being with her that night had been eye-opening. No games. No false promises. Just a good time and a night he would never forget. After the hell of his divorce, she'd been just what he'd needed.

"You said you worked here," he said.

"I do." She spread her hands. "As you see."

He looked around at the frou-frou spa stuff and listened for a second to the almost-imperceptible music playing overhead. There were a lot of hearts here too, like in Cypress. It seemed like he couldn't escape the holiday, even here on Crescent Key. Too bad Billy couldn't get Shannon to come here with him. Instead he was here as a surrogate, and as alone as he'd ever been.

"Shannon worked here too," he said.

She blew out a breath. "Why are you here, Chase?"

He blinked. "I told you."

"You're here for Billy. Yeah, you told me." She crossed her arms. "But why are you *here*? At the spa?"

He quirked a smile at her. "Can't you take a guess?"

She shook her head. "Oh no, you don't. You're not doing that dimpled-smile seduction thing again."

He blinked at her. "That dimpled what?"

She waved a hand. "Never mind. It's just so not going to happen."

He shrugged. "I wanted to see you."

She snorted, and then covered her mouth. "It's been over a month, Chase. No calls or texts."

"We didn't exchange numbers."

"All right. No messages on Facebook, then."

"I thought you wanted to…"

"Hit it and quit it?" she provided.

His mouth dropped open. "Not exactly, but you didn't seem like you wanted that night to be anything more than what it was."

Her brows drew together. "You're not wrong there."

"Then what's changed?"

She appeared so worried by his question now that he thought he'd lighten the moment and fast.

"Don't tell me you can't wait for another taste of Chase?" he teased.

Her mouth dropped open and then she laughed. "I'm not going to touch that ridiculous line."

She was on the ball. Spunky. He'd noticed her quick mind that night, but he hadn't paid much attention to it. No. He'd been too busy thinking about her quick hands.

"When are you finished here?" he asked.

She gaped at him. "When?"

"Today, Carrie. When are you finished here today?"

"Why?"

He leaned against the sales counter and shook his head. "I was only asking you to come to dinner with me, Red."

"Dinner." Now her cheeks flushed a pretty pink that nearly matched the sweet little freckles marching across the bridge of her nose. "Just dinner?"

20

He smiled again, risking that dimple comment if it got her to thaw a little bit. "Sure."

She nibbled her plump bottom lip and his mind went back to how delectable her mouth was. Hell, her *everything* was pretty delicious.

"Yeah," she said. "We can do dinner."

She looked so serious that he almost let her off the hook. Almost. He wanted to see if that electricity they'd experienced the night of the wedding was a fluke. It had sure been unlike anything he'd ever experienced.

"Seeing as I'm staying right here at the Crescent Resort, why don't we eat here?

***

Carrie stared at Chase for a long minute. Oh, could she do this? Sit down to a meal with this guy? She was really tempted. He looked at her with those deep hazel eyes and she flashed back to that night out by the lake. He was tall and broad, and even more handsome than Shannon's Billy Goat. Those shoulders stretching his gray Henley shirt. Those long, strong legs clad in worn jeans. He wore sneakers and appeared very casual, but she could so picture him as he'd looked in his dark suit back then. Crisp white shirt. Loosened tie. Even his hands were beautiful. And oh, what those hands had felt like on her skin.

He had issues though, which he'd revealed yet again when he'd mentioned his own wedding. Once more, those darn blue lines flashed in her mind. He had a right to know. There were no ifs, ands or buts about it. She had to tell him what was going on.

"Okay, Chase." She smiled up at him. "Dinner sounds good."

The grin that spread across his face nearly took her breath. "Great. Listen, you know this place inside and out. You pick the restaurant. When can I pick you up?"

Anytime, apparently. "I'm done here at five so, six?"

He nodded. "Six it is."

He left the spa shop and Carrie sank back against the counter. She was having dinner with the hottest guy she'd ever been with. Heck, the hottest guy she'd ever seen. She might have bought into Doug's lines, but that was so last year. This year she had a new life coming, in more ways than one. She'd been so sure of it. That was why she'd jumped all over Chase at Shannon's wedding. It had been so out of character for her it had seemed like a dream. A gift for her wounded pride and self-esteem. A gift that apparently kept on giving.

She covered her midriff with one hand, taking in a deep breath. She could still smell Chase, that hot fresh scent she'd caught at first and reveled in later. And now she had to face the fact that the one time in her life she let herself go would have lasting consequences.

"Wow, he's hot."

Carrie looked over at Spiky-hair. "Yeah, he is."

"So what's your story?" Today's spa receptionist looked at her with bright eyes. "You know. With him?"

He's my baby-daddy. Carrie waved a hand. "No story, really. We're going out to dinner tonight."

"Where?"

"I'm not sure."

The other girl's pierced left eyebrow shot up to her hairline. "Wisteria?"

Carrie shook her head. "No way. That place is too expensive. Besides, it's full of expectations on a plate."

"And the best food at Crescent."

"Yeah, well maybe we'll just hit the poolside bar." She winced as she remembered that Doug's latest still worked there. "Never mind. Maybe Mexican."

The entrance doors of the spa opened with an audible *whoosh* and the girl jumped a little. "Gotta run."

She dashed through the archway and back to her desk. Carrie just nodded as she was once more alone in the spa shop. Maybe this one would stick. Next time maybe she would pay attention to the girl's name tag.

Spiky-hair was right, though. Wisteria was the best restaurant at the resort but it was also the most popular. Cozy and intimate, and very date-y. She wasn't ready to date Chase. That should be funny, since she'd already slept with him.

"So you're going to the Rancho Casa?" Marion asked.

Carrie looked over at her boss. Rancho Casa, was the little Mexican restaurant that was very popular with locals. It was small and always busy. Right now, the thought of their silky-soft *tamales* made her mouth water.

"I guess so. Chase wants to go to dinner."

"Chase?"

"Chase Harris."

"Harris? Is he related to Billy?"

Carrie managed a nod. "His cousin."

Marion's eyes narrowed. "And you know him how, exactly?"

Carrie's face heated. "I met him at the wedding."

"Aha!"

"What does that mean?"

"He's the reason your spirits looked quite restored when you came back."

"Quite restored?" Carrie wrinkled her nose. "Have I taken a tonic?"

"I don't know." Marion winked. "Have you?"

Carrie kept her expression even until Marion laughed lightly.

"Okay, I'll stop," she said. "It's nice to see that spunk again, though."

Her boss returned to the spa and Carrie went about the routine of straightening and readying the shop for the next day. As she did so, she thought about what Marion had said.

Spunk? The woman was wrong about that. Carrie hadn't felt all that spunky since finding out about Doug and bartender-girl at Thanksgiving. She'd love the jerk, and foolishly believed him every darn time he'd said he loved her back. He hadn't. Not enough to keep it in his pants, anyway.

Then Chase had walked into the wedding reception on New Year's Eve. The setting had been gorgeous, and so different from what she'd seen during her childhood growing up on the gulf in Tampa. There had been a white tent set up on the sandy, leaf-strewn soil between towering oaks and Cypress trees dripping with Spanish moss. Fairy lights had been strung on everything that didn't move. Music and laughter and alcohol had filled the space. It had been just what she'd needed to wake from the funk she'd wallowed in since Doug.

She'd been thrilled for her friend, too. How could she not be? Shannon had married the man she was supposed to be with. Her Billy Goat. Marion was right about that. It had been as clear as crystal when Shannon taken off her shoes and dipped her toes in the sand. Carrie had dropped more than her shoes on that night with Chase. Her insecurities, her inhibitions. A flush of heat washed over her. Her dress.

The next morning she'd felt amazing. Complete somehow, and more like herself than ever. It had been like she'd woken up. Marion called it spunk, and Carrie reasoned she could own that. Tonight she had to rouse that spunk and fast.

Tonight she had to tell Chase he was going to be a father.

Chapter 3

Chase didn't think the restaurant looked very promising from outside, but the small parking lot was packed. Carrie had assured him it was the best Mexican restaurant around and, after reading the chalk-board specials menu and being shown to a small table in the center of the crowded dining room, he was inclined to believe her.

The air was scented with spices and heat and cheese, and his mouth watered. Of course, part of the reason for that could be the gorgeous girl sitting across from him. She still wore her crisp white blouse, but had added a thin pink sweater. She'd apparently done some comb and flip thing with her hair. God, he loved her hair.

At the wedding, he'd noticed it from the jump. Red shoulder-length waves that caught the glimmer from the fairy lights strung overhead. He'd fisted it in his hands when they'd been alone after, holding on to the silken strands as he'd lost himself for the first time in my memory. And in the morning her scent, something flowery and soft, had filled his head as he'd woken up with his face buried in her hair.

Tonight she'd ditched the headband he'd seen earlier and the strands looked shiny and soft once more in the light from the hanging fixture above them. They were seated at a small round table for two, and the setting was surprisingly intimate despite how many diners surrounded them.

"This looks like a very popular place," he said.

"The food is fantastic."

He nodded. "I saw the specials board. Looks like there's a ton of choices. What do you suggest?"

"I'm diving into the *tamales*." She fiddled with her cloth napkin. "You?"

"Something with meat. *Carne Asada*, I think."

She seemed a little uneasy, but he felt that too. They'd hardly talked on the night they'd hooked up. Just a few lines and some smiles and he'd been on her like he needed her kisses to live.

A male server stopped at their table with two glasses of water and they placed their meal orders. Chase couldn't resist adding a couple of *tamales* himself, and finished his order with a bottle of Corona.

"What are you drinking?" he asked Carrie.

"Frozen Margarita." She gasped. "Oh! Just iced tea, please. Sweet."

The server left and Chase looked at her. She was back to fiddling with her napkin.

"Why didn't you get a drink?" he asked.

She gave a quick shake of her head. "No reason. Long day. Work tomorrow."

"I'm off for the next week." Their drinks came and he lifted his beer bottle. "Although when I get back, I might be working for Billy instead of at the ranch."

"You work at a ranch?"

"My family's ranch, actually."

"So you're a cowboy?"

He smiled. "Not technically. We raise cattle."

"Is that why Billy wants his own farm?"

Chase thought for a second. "I guess so. My brother and I...we weren't very kind to Billy growing up."

That was the first time he'd ever admitted that to anybody outside the family. His stomach churned as he recalled just how cold he'd been to his orphaned cousin.

"But you're close now." She sipped her iced tea. "I saw that at the wedding."

Chase shrugged. "I have a lot of making up to do. Helping Billy out like this? It's the least I can do."

"What about your brother?"

His brother. His older brother, Zach. He was even more bull-headed than Chase.

"Zach can make it up in his own way if he wants to."

Her brows drew together. "I'm an only child."

"Yeah?" He folded his arms and leaned on the table. "What's that like?"

A smile curved her lips and warmth came into her eyes. "It was great, actually. My parents live up in Tampa, still happy after more than thirty years of marriage."

He whistled. "That's a long time."

"What about your parents?"

A chill gripped his belly. "My mom took off when I was eight."

Her lips parted. "Oh. I'm sorry."

He brushed her concern with a shrug, setting aside the long-held feeling of abandonment. The woman had run off with an equipment salesman, as clichéd as that might be. She'd snuck off while the boys had been at school. That was not a day Chase wanted to dwell on, thanks.

"My father provided for us," he said. "We worked the ranch, sure. But we never went without."

"And he left money to Billy when he died." Chase arched a brow and she smiled. "Shannon told me."

"I don't begrudge Billy one penny. Wild Harry Harris wasn't a touchy-feely kind of guy. I guess he loved Billy as much as he loved me and my brother Zach. Not a one of us really saw it, though."

"That's a shame."

"It is what it is."

He took a long pull on his beer. Talking about Wild Harry was always difficult, and now that he was seriously considering getting out of the ranch entirely? He just didn't want to deal with it right now. He missed his father, despite their distant relationship.

He was grateful when their food came, and it looked as good as it smelled. His stomach growled and he grinned. "You weren't kidding about this place, were you?"

She nodded and unfolded the wrapping on her tamale. Breathing in, she closed her eyes and sighed. "Oh, I've been craving this."

His body tightened as he saw the pleasure dance across her face. Then he started to eat and any other appetites were shoved to the back of his mind as the tender seasoned beef of his *carne asada* filled his mouth.

"Oh my God," he mumbled. "Man."

She shot him a cheeky grin. "Told you."

They ate, talking about the wedding but not what had happened after the reception. He wasn't expecting any sort of rehash of what was arguably his best night with a woman. He wasn't so modest as to think he hadn't rung her bells a couple of times too. He was a gentleman, however.

Wild Harry might have been a semi-distracted single father but he'd never spoken of a woman without a respectful tone. Except for Chase's mother, of course. Of her, he'd never spoken at all.

"Would you like another beer?" the server asked after a few minutes.

He shook his head. "No, thanks. More water would be great, though."

"How about dessert?"

Chase didn't want to head back to his ridiculously luxurious guest room at Crescent yet, and dessert was a pretty good diversion.

Carrie bit her lower lip as she apparently considered the server's question. "Hmm. *Sopapillas*, I think. With chocolate sauce for dipping."

"Or something," Chase couldn't help but add.

The server chuckled but left to put in their order.

"You're naughty, Chase Harris," Carrie said.

"Not me. I'm just a normal, red-blooded guy."

She tilted her head to one side, her eyes narrowed. "Of that, I'm not so sure."

***

Carrie wasn't sure why she's said that, but she'd sensed there was more to Chase Harris than he let on. He presented the picture of a carefree country boy, but she'd seen the hurt flitter across his face as he'd touched on the subject of his mother.

Dessert soon arrived, crisp fried chips of sugar-and-cinnamon dusted dough and a small bowl of fragrant melted chocolate sauce. Her senses sparked and she let out a little moan.

She heard Chase chuckle and met his gaze. "What?"

"That sound, Red. That's all I've been thinking about since seeing you again this afternoon."

Of that, she was inclined to believe him. She had no clue what was going through his mind at this moment, either. He probably wanted to hook up again. If she were honest, she was seriously considering indulging in some moan-inducing behavior too. It was so out of character for her, as anything involving this guy was. It had to be her hormones.

Choosing to ignore the tempting man seated across from her, she dug in to their dessert and drowned her senses in sugar, grease and chocolate. Chase watched her for a minute longer and then joined her.

Groaning, he wiped his mouth. "Damn, that's good. Maybe keeping the chocolate sauce on the table is a good thing. For now."

She smiled as she licked the cinnamon sugar from her lips. "This dessert makes me feel like a kid. Like I'm eating donut holes or something."

He nodded. "Yeah, just about the only thing that brought the Harris men together was when one of the women from church brought pies and cakes over to the ranch."

"Let me guess. They were hoping to become your new mother, right?"

Chase snorted. "You're probably right. Wild Harry never dated a one of them, not that I or Zach or Billy ever knew. He was pretty torn up over my mother."

Here was an opening for her delicate conversation. He was talking about his childhood. His parents.

"You missed her a lot too, didn't you."

"Not at all."

She pulled back a little. "Seriously?"

His eyes darkened nearly to a shade of brown as deep as the sauce left in the bowl between them. "She left us, Carrie. Me and Zach and our father. She never looked back, either. How could a parent do that?"

Instinctively, her hand strayed to her midsection. "I can't imagine doing any such thing."

He blew out a breath. "I'll tell you this, it's a damn good thing I never had kids with my ex."

"Was your breakup that contentious?"

He leveled a look at her that was so cold she nearly flinched. "She left me like my mother did. Took up with another guy."

"She cheated on you?"

"She said she didn't. Said she fell in love."

Carrie's mouth dropped open. "Oh, that sucks."

He laughed without any humor she could see. "Yeah, but I'm better off. She sure as hell is."

"How long were you married?"

"Just under two years. It was a cluster fuck from the start."

She blinked at him. "You weren't in love?"

"Hell, no. We'd hook up once in a while and then she got pregnant."

Carrie jerked a little but managed to keep her face impassive. "I thought you said you didn't have any kids."

"No, we didn't. Turned out she only thought she was pregnant. Why the hell we stayed together after she found out it was just some hormonal thing? I have no idea."

"Maybe you loved her more than you thought."

"Yeah. And maybe I was delusional." He spread his hands. "Look, I know marriage works for some people. I'm praying it works for Billy and Shannon, and it looks like it just might. Me? I'm just not built for happy endings."

Her heart sank. How could she tell this man that he was going to be a father when he so clearly had no interest in any kind of future? Not with a wife and certainly not with a child.

Suddenly the tamales, and the crisp and sugary dessert, churned in her belly. Pushing her dish away, she sat back. He seemed to take that as some sort of signal, and raised his hand to the server. After settling their bill, he waved her ahead of him to his truck parked on the darkened street.

"This was really nice," she said for lack of anything else to say.

"I'm glad we did this."

He seemed to have lost that prickliness she'd seen as he'd talked about his failed marriage. In fact, he walked with an ease of movement that showcased his very fit body. *Hello, hormones.* She was seized with the want she'd felt at the wedding.

The drive back to Crescent didn't take very long, and by the time they parked she had made up her mind. She had to tell him. It was unconscionable to have this information and not tell him. Earlier she'd had the excuse of dinner in a public place, but now they were cocooned in the leather-seated luxury of his truck.

"Chase, I have something to tell you," she began.

"Okay." He turned, one arm propped on the steering wheel and his body angled towards her. "Shoot."

She opened her mouth, but the words wouldn't come. He quirked a very sexy smile in her direction and brought his face close to hers.

"We don't have to talk, Red." He clicked out of his seatbelt and came closer still to brush his sculpted lips over hers. "To my thinking? There's a whole lot more we can do."

Oh, this man was so dangerous. She wanted to cuddle up against him and breathe deeply of his scent that surrounded her. She wanted to throw herself into his arms like she'd done before and think about the consequences later.

"That night, Chase. The night of the wedding." She touched his face and drove her fingers through his thick brown waves. "That was the first time I've ever done that."

"Yeah?" He buzzed her lips again and grinned. "You have to be more specific about that night, Carrie. We did a lot of things, to my recollection."

Heat flashed over her, and she suspected her face was as red as her hair. That night had been such a departure for her. Chase did something to her head as well as her body, and she had indulged every naughty thought she'd ever had with his very willing self.

"I meant hook up, Chase. That's just not me."

"There's no shame in that, Red." He held her closer, and she realized he'd undone her seatbelt as well. "We're both unattached." His lips ran over her throat and she tilted her head back. "We both like making each other feel good."

"Y-yes." She shivered as his tongue stroked over her skin. "But I have to tell you something."

"We can talk after," he said, his voice low and rough.

She closed her eyes and gathered the strength to pull back from him. "Chase, please."

He grumbled but his crooked smile told her he was being playful. "Okay, Red. Shoot."

She stared into his eyes and took a deep breath. "Chase, I'm pregnant."

Chapter 4

Chase pulled back as if Carrie had punched him square in the jaw. His belly clenched and he couldn't seem to catch his breath.

"You're pregnant?" he managed to ask on a whisper.

Carrie was staring at him, her eyes wide as she nodded. "Yes." She bit her bottom lip. "I took the test this morning."

He sat back, gripping the steering wheel so hard the leather wrapping crackled in his hands. "You're pregnant." He looked at her out of the corner of his eye. "You're sure?"

She gave a shaky nod. "I was pretty certain for the last couple of weeks, and the test confirmed it."

His mind swirled with so many thoughts he had no clue what he should say to her now. Cheyanne hadn't taken a test, yet Chase had insisted they get married. If he thought too long about it, he was sure it was all tied up with his mother's abandonment when he was a kid or some shit like that.

He'd pushed Cheyanne to get married and they had. His ex-wife had pushed to get divorced, and they had. Now he was faced with another woman saying he was going to be a father. But this time, the woman was sure of it.

"You want to get married?" he asked. She gasped and he faced her fully. "What?"

"Are you serious? That's what you think this is?"

"What do you mean?"

"You think I'm telling you this because of the story you told me about your marriage?" Her eyes snapped at him. "How you got married because…because…"

He shook his head. "No, I don't think you told me because of what I said. I think you're sure."

"Well, that's something." She blew out a breath. "You seriously want to get married? We don't even know each other."

"Maybe, but I know we get along. In and out of bed. That already gives our marriage a better chance than mine every had."

She held up a hand. "We get along? We laughed and danced at a wedding, fell into bed together, and tonight we shared one meal."

"Exactly."

"Exactly?" She sat as far back in her seat as she apparently could manage. "You're delusional."

He knew he had to take a step back. Put her at ease somehow. But the thought of a child of his growing up without him made his head spin.

"Okay, you're right. We don't really know each other. Not yet, anyway."

She clicked her tongue. "Uh, yeah."

"Why don't we do that, then?"

Her eyes narrowed on him. "Do *what*, then?"

He forced ease in his posture as he flashed her a smile. "Get to know each other, Red. Date."

Her lush mouth dropped open and he longed for another kiss. Licking his lips, he reined in the sharp desire he only seemed to have for this particular woman.

"You want to date?"

"Are you having trouble processing, Carrie?" He winked. "I know I can have that effect on you."

She covered her face with her hands and then ran her fingers through her hair. She seemed to be steeling herself, and he readied for a quick refusal. A simple dismissal. To his surprise and relief, she nodded.

"Okay. We can date."

He fist-bumped the dashboard. "Yes!" That earned him a small smile that eased the tension in the truck cab in a big way. "I'm here for a week, Carrie. I'd say that's just about long enough to figure this thing out."

"A week is long enough? If you say so. Now, I'm going to say goodnight."

He cupped her face and gave her a sweet, lingering kiss. It would have to be enough for tonight. "Where are you parked?"

"Right there." She indicated a small hybrid parked three spaces away. "I don't have a long drive home. I live just around the corner from the Crisscross."

He arched a brow. "The Crisscross?"

Her smile widened. "Don't even start. It's the Crisscross Motel. I'll have you know that is an historical landmark."

"Let me guess. The site of a famous murder-for-hire?"

"Ha. No, it's names for the very first intersection on Crescent Key. And it's just a few miles away from Crescent."

"Okay."

She tilted her head to one side, her eyes sparkling. "Chase Harris, are you worried about me?"

"I'm a gentleman, Red. My father might have been a little distant, but he raised me right in the respect department."

She nodded. "Yeah, I see that. I saw it with Billy too. He has this kind of nobility, somehow."

Chase acknowledged her words with a nod. His cousin was a good guy, and if Chase gave off a little bit of that vibe? Cool.

"Well, I'm grateful for the comparison," he said.

She opened her door but before she could step down he got out himself and hurried around to her side. She smiled at him and grabbed her bag off the truck floor. "Thanks again for dinner, Chase."

"Sure thing." He leaned on the door frame and held out a hand. "Give me your phone?"

Her brow furrowed but she did so. He put his info into her contacts and handed it back. "I'll text you tomorrow, Carrie."

She slid the phone back in her purse. "Okay." She gazed at him for a beat. "Until tomorrow."

He watched her get into her little car and didn't stop watching until she'd turned out of the parking lot. She didn't have a very long drive, she'd said. From what he'd seen Crescent Key was pretty small. Hell, they considered an intersection historical. He guessed nobody had a very long drive to get anywhere.

As he locked the truck and walked towards the lobby of the resort, he thought about everything that had happened tonight. He'd been attracted to Carrie from the jump, and spending a little more time in her company—upright in her company, this time— that feeling only intensified. She'd been easy to talk to. So easy, that he'd spilled the crap that was his marriage. Then she'd spilled something that could change his entire world.

He nodded to the girl working the front desk and headed up to his guest room on the second floor. Letting himself inside, he crossed to the wide glass doors framing the balcony. He slid one of the doors open and stepped out. The balcony was huge, and gave him a view like a picture postcard of the gulf at night. A big fat moon hung over the water and cast ripples of light on the gentle waves below. The water lapped at the shore, and no one stood on the sand that he could see. He could almost believe he was the only man in the world, staring out at that water. He wasn't, though. Not even close.

Carrie was pregnant. He was going to be a father for real this time. She'd teased him about worrying about her. Was he worried about her? Damn right, he was. She didn't know it, but she held more than his baby in her belly.

She held any chance he had at having a real family in her hands.

***

Carrie woke on Thursday morning, her stomach queasy and a headache thrumming behind her eyes. She sat on the edge of her bed, taking in slow deep breaths until everything seemed to settle.

A visit to the bathroom for a splash of cool water on her face sent any discomfort more fully to the corners of her consciousness.

She stared into the mirror for a long minute, pulling her hair away from her face. She didn't look any different, considering the ridiculous upheaval of the previous day. She'd had to face the truth on that plastic stick tossed into the small trashcan beneath the chunky fifties wall-mounted pink sink. Then she'd had to tell the baby daddy, although she hadn't thought that would have to happen for weeks if not months. She'd never expected him to walk into the spa shop, let alone ask her to dinner.

"He asked me to marry him," she murmured. "Jeez."

She took a quick shower standing in the thick porcelain tub, also pink, and returned to her room to dress for work. When Doug had ended things he'd kept the apartment they'd shared for seven months. His name was on the lease, he'd pointed out. Since he'd been banging the bartender girl Brandi in the bed they'd also shared, she'd moved out in December without any argument. Thank goodness Marion Tucker had stepped in with this offer of a quaint second-story efficiency apartment.

Shannon had lived here last summer, but the apartment didn't show any of her personal touches. Billy had swept her off her feet, kicked-off shoes and all, too quickly for her to leave any stamp on the place. Neat as a pin, it bore the landlady's handiwork down to the crocheted afghan blanketing the big soft floral sofa in the living space.

Mrs. Battle and her husband were both very dear, and the older woman snuck in every few days to tidy things up. It made Carrie feel a little bit homesick for her mom's sometimes intrusive but always caring touch. Carrie finished dressing and went into the kitchen to grab something for breakfast.

Grabbing a bottled yogurt drink out of the fridge, she cracked it open and took a sip. Her nausea seemed to be gone, but she didn't want to risk anything more than this in her stomach this morning. How she'd wolfed down those *tamales* and *sopapillas* last night, she wasn't sure.

Along with the curved fifties fridge and chrome trimmed dinette set, the rest of the apartment carried through the vibe seen in the pink-tiled bathroom. No, Carrie's home was like a time capsule. Walnut furniture polished to a high sheen. A console TV like she vaguely remembered her grandparents having. This one had a record player tucked down inside. It was all so homey and just what she'd needed when her relationship with Doug had imploded.

She dressed for a day at work. Serenity Spa was busiest during the week, with bridal parties getting ready for the big event and just a few couples and singles taking advantage of the spa's treatment options. Thursdays and Fridays could be hopping.

The adjacent shop's hours mirrored the spa's, and Carrie looked forward to Saturday when she would only work a half-day. She wasn't the only one on staff, and Marion usually had one of the fill-in receptionists cover the shop during the slow Saturday afternoon. As for Sundays, Marion insisted one full weekend day off was necessary for both the body and mind. Carrie appreciated it, and knew that at least one reason was the adorable baby waiting at home for Marion and her husband.

A baby. She glanced down at her belly and marveled that there was a life growing there. Her child. Chase Harris's child. She owed it to her baby to get to know its father better. Jeez, he'd asked her to marry him!

"Yeah, right. That's just what I need to do right now. Jump into a marriage as quickly as I'd jumped into a relationship with Doug the Slug."

The nickname made her smile a little as she locked up and went down to her car. The drive to Crescent was short, like she'd told Chase last night. He'd been worried about her, or about the baby at least. It was nice, having someone other than her family worrying over her. Unease caused a flutter in her belly. She couldn't get used to this. Chase was just floored by her abruptly-delivered news. His knee-jerk marriage proposal was too insane to consider.

As she breezed through the sumptuous, Victorian-inspired lobby she ignored the lure of the coffee shop. There was a line forming, which she also ignored. She did take in a deep breath, though. Mmm, nothing smelled better than a coffee shop on a busy morning.

"Hey, there!" a woman's voice called.

Carrie looked over to see Spiky-hair waving and walked over. Ignoring the dirty looks from the tall skinny guy standing behind her, she lifted her chin. "Hey…"

"Paula," the other woman said. "Get you a coffee?"

Carrie nibbled her bottom lip. "Um, no. I shouldn't."

Spiky-hair, Paula as Carrie knew now, gave a sage nod. "Cutting down?"

"Cutting out," Carrie said without thinking.

Paula blinked at her. "I could never do such a thing. Don't let the blond spikes fool you. I'm half-Columbian. Coffee runs in my veins."

"How do you sleep at night?" Carrie asked.

Paula laughed. "Right?"

Carrie patted her arm. "I guess I'll see you at Serenity."

"Yep." Paula blew out a breath. "If this line ever moves."

Carrie shrugged and turned towards the spa. And right into the broad chest of Chase Harris himself.

"Morning, Red."

She tilted her head back to stare up into his very handsome face. He'd shaved that lovely stubble she'd felt on her skin last night, and she wasn't sure which image was more attractive. He wore another yummy Henley, this one in dark green, with just the right number of buttons undone and the sleeves pushed up on his forearms. Her breath caught but she fought the urge to snuggle against him for just a second. He smelled even better than the coffee shop did.

"Good morning, Chase."

"I was going to offer to get you a coffee, but maybe you want tea instead?"

She held up a hand. "No, thanks. I'm good."

"So how about lunch today?"

She slanted him a look. "It's not even nine o'clock."

"Hey, I'm a guy with a plan. I've only got one week, remember."

One week. That unease came again, and she placed a hand on his chest. Oh, he had a very nice chest. "And I'm a girl who has to get to work."

He covered her hand with his and it felt so right. She could almost feel his heart beating beneath her palm. Forcing herself to slide her hand free, she took a step back.

"You're serious about this." She wasn't asking him a question. "You want to see where this goes."

He nodded, crossing his arms. "I do. I think we owe it to…ourselves." His eyes flicked to her midsection for a second before pinning her again with their mossy green-brown depths. "Don't you?"

"Yes," she admitted. "Okay, lunch."

His smile was bright and nearly knocked her off of her feet. "I'll come by the shop later, Red." He winked. "Count on it."

With that he headed into the coffee shop. She turned and took measured steps towards the spa shop.

Count on it. If she were being honest, she wanted to. She doubted he was as good as he seemed. She'd fallen for Doug the Slug, hadn't she?

Nevertheless, she'd agreed to date Chase for one week. That she could count on. As for hoping for more than that?

She'd be a fool to believe they could be anything more than a one-night mistake.

Chapter 5

Chase sat in the coffee shop, nursing a simple Americano coffee. He'd noticed the bake case full of heart-shaped cookies and pink-frosted pastries, though. Valentine's Day was Sunday, after all. Maybe he could use that to his advantage with Carrie?

She'd seemed really prickly this morning. Maybe she wasn't feeling well? He'd seen the interest in her pretty blue eyes as her gaze had traveled over the front of him, though. She was still attracted to him, which boded well for his cause. He wanted to be a part of their baby's life, a big part if he could manage it, and reminding its mother of their compatibility and attraction just might be the beginning of something greater.

His phone dinged with a message and he drew it out of his jean's pocket. He had a text from Jo Potter.

I'll be at Crescent this afternoon. Can u meet?

He texted back his answer in the affirmative.

See you at Serenity around 1? she texted in return.

Sounds good.

Setting his phone on the table, he took another sip of his very plain, very perfect coffee. One o'clock at Serenity would be perfect, too. He would just be bringing Carrie back to work after their lunch. He leaned back in his chair, his arms crossed. He was dating, apparently. The mother of his baby, actually. He was so out of his element, but he'd be damned if he let his discomfort show.

He'd never dated Cheyanne. Even after she'd told him she suspected she was pregnant. No, like an idiot he'd put out a marriage proposal that seemed to shock her as much as it had him. And being as stubborn as one of his father's meanest bulls, he'd dug in his heels and pushed forward with the wedding even after she'd told him it was a false alarm.

Carrie was sure, though. She'd said as much, even though she hadn't been to a doctor yet. Maybe he should tell her to make an appointment.

"Yeah," he grumbled to himself. "That would go over real big."

"Mister Harris, I presume?" a tall, dark-haired woman asked. She stood in front of him, holding a cardboard cup of coffee.

Chase nodded and straightened in his chair. "That's me. Chase Harris, actually."

The woman smiled and stuck out her free hand. "Marion Tucker."

Chase's mind worked as he stood. "Tucker." It hit him then, the memory of some of the stuff Billy had told him. He gave her hand a shake before releasing her. "You run Serenity."

She laughed softly. "Yes, that's me in a nutshell. And you're dating Carrie Boyles."

"Boyles," he repeated. "I…yeah, that's right."

She tilted her head. "Didn't you know her last name?"

His face grew hot but he tamped down any embarrassment. "I guess it didn't come up."

"I'll give you one thing, Chase. You're honest."

"To a fault, my father used to say."

Chase didn't know where that particular nugget had come from, but it was indeed something Wild Harry used to tell him. A little discretion would have saved Chase a few schoolyard beatings and a couple of parent-teacher conferences. That was true.

Marion crossed her arms and nodded. "Good. Carrie could use some honesty in her life right now."

When Chase opened his mouth to ask her just what she was talking about, the woman held up one hand.

"Nope. Not my story to tell," she went on. "Maybe Carrie will let you know just what Doug the Slug did to her behind her back. Maybe she won't."

Chase didn't need to hear more. Clearly Carrie's ex had fooled around on her. Had he broken her heart? That was the million-dollar question.

"Then I'm her guy, I think," he said.

Marion grinned. "Good." She reached out to place a hand on his arm. "Don't hurt her. If you do? You can't run fast enough or far enough to keep me from getting even."

Chase brushed off her threat with a shrug. "I have no intention of hurting her."

Her eyes narrowed. "You know, I believe you. You have that honest Harris thing going on."

Chase found a smile. "I take it my cousin made quite an impression last summer."

"He sure did. He stole away one of my two favorite employees, too. Can you guess who the other one is?"

Chase grinned himself now. "I believe I can."

"Good." She raised her cup in his direction. "Have a good day, Chase Harris."

"You, too."

She nodded and then took brisk steps out of the coffee shop, her heels clicking on the tile floor as she made her way across the lobby.

Chase's mind worked around what Carrie's boss had said as he sat back down. She was putting him on his guard. There was really no need, even though a lot of what she said was true.

He really didn't know much about Carrie. Hell, he hadn't even known her last name when he'd jumped in and asked her to change it just last night. He had to be careful going forward. He wanted some kind of future with her, and didn't want to do anything to screw that up.

Tossing his empty coffee cup in the nearest trash can, he crossed the lobby himself. He avoided the spa's attractive, arched entry of frosted glass, though. He didn't want to seem like a stalker. Popping in to check on Carrie would definitely be a misstep right now.

Instead he made his way over to the concierge desk. Nodding absently at the neat tall man behind the counter, he looked through the brochures tucked into the clear plastic stand set to one side. There seemed to be a lot to do on Crescent Key, from dinner cruises to boat rentals and surfing lessons. None of these really appealed much to him. He wasn't much of a water rat.

Being pulled behind a motor boat in a tube was the extent of his watersports experience. Long afternoons out on the lake, mostly with a beer in his hand, were something he and Zach had shared. Never with Billy, though. And certainly never with their father.

Truth was, he had more to mend than just his almost-relationship with Carrie. More than his kinship with Billy. He and Zach hadn't really talked since Wild Harry died, and they disagreed over just about everything related to the ranch.

A brochure caught his eye, announcing the coming attractions to the area. A soccer complex, a tourist center and petting zoo, including a working goat farm. That was what Billy wanted to bring to Cypress.

Maybe Chase could get to know more about that from Jo Potter herself. He knew today's meeting would most likely be a short one, but he did have a week here in Serenity Shores. Maybe he'd spend some time out at her farm and get to know more about the business.

At the very least, it would help keep him from pressing Carrie for too much too soon.

***

Carrie smiled at the customer in front of her as she handed her a bag full of soaps and candles. Valentine's Day was Sunday, and clearly the grinning guy had big plans for his sweetheart. She tried not to let it bother her. She'd been single for last year's lovers' holiday, hadn't she? She'd lived through that without any problem. Little had she known what she would go through over the past year since then.

First Doug the Slug convinced her that he loved her. Heck, he'd convinced her that she'd loved him too. They'd started dating in March and by the end of April they'd been living together. Rushing into things hadn't been the right thing to do. She'd suspected that then, yet she'd ignored her instincts and jumped into a serious relationship with Doug. And now this thing with Chase, whatever it was, made her feel like she was moving at light speed.

He'd given her one week. What did that mean, exactly? He seemed like the kind of guy who wasn't exactly patient. Then again, maybe she'd misjudged him. He was kind of sweet under all that intensity. Lord knew he was the hottest guy she'd ever met.

"Almost time for lunch."

She looked over at Paula and smiled. "And this afternoon you get to come in here, right?"

"Shadowing you, you mean?" At Carrie's nod, Paula shrugged. "Hey, I'm up for diversifying my skillset."

"Smart girl."

The spa doors slid open and Paula hurried out of the shop to return to her desk. Carrie straightened a little bit and then walked over to the archway to turn the standing sign around to read "closed." As she straightened she saw that Chase stood in the spa reception area.

"Ready for lunch, Red?" he asked.

Carrie's pulse kicked at the sight of him. At the sound of his voice, actually. Paula stared between the two of them, her eyes round.

Carrie nodded, choosing to ignore the questions raised by Paula's pierced brows. "Sure. Just let me grab my bag."

When she stood behind the sales counter, her purse over her shoulder, she took a deep calming breath.

"It's just lunch," she told herself. "Deal, already."

Feeling a little bit bolstered by her short pep talk, she was smiling when she rejoined Chase.

"How about lunch out by the pool?" he asked.

Carrie's heart skittered to a stop and then began to race. "No, I don't think so."

Chase stared at her for a beat. "Okay. I just thought that it would be quicker for you."

Carrie looked over at Paula, who was still staring at Chase with one brow raised. No help there, then.

"Sure. That's fine," Carrie said. "And very considerate of you."

Chase dipped his head, his sparkling eyes tilted up at her from beneath his brows. "Anything to please the lady."

Paula sighed audibly and Carrie shook her head. She couldn't really blame her. Chase Harris was very delectable right now, all testosterone and gentlemanly manners. She would just suck it up and risk seeing Doug's latest buzzing around the poolside bar.

The day was temperate, with just a hint of a chill in the breeze coming off of the gulf. The bar was situated right beside the pool, and the lush surrounding landscaping led the eye towards the adjacent beach. This view was one of Carrie's favorites. She and Doug had spent lots of evenings hanging out in the casual dining place, though now she suspected that one of the reasons was Brandi, the bartender.

He'd been very friendly with the woman. Always talking to her. Flirting with her. Carrie had just chalked it up to Doug's personality. To his job as a salesman. Wow, had she been blind.

"This place looks pretty good," Chase said as they neared the bar. "What do you want for lunch?"

"I could go for a burger," she answered.

Her hunger quickly diminished as she spotted the dark-haired woman who stepped up to greet them at the makeshift hostess area at one end of the bar. Brandi's brown eyes widened as she recognized Carrie.

"Oh." The woman cleared her throat. "Hey."

Carrie couldn't make herself speak. This was the woman Doug had left her for, even before he'd actually left her. *Ugh.*

The bartender gazed up at Chase, her eyes narrowed. "You look familiar."

Carrie found her voice. "This is Chase Harris."

Brandi slapped her hand on the bar, a small smile on her lips. "Billy Goat! Man, do you look a lot like him. Is he your brother?"

"Cousin," Chase said, placing his hands on Carrie's shoulders. "We'd like to order a couple of burgers, please. We'll be sitting over there."

Clearly the guy caught the tension between her and Doug's girlfriend. Brandi blinked and gave a shaky nod. "Sure."

Carrie hurried away from the bar to a table set not far from the beach. Chase reached for her chair but she sat before he could do more of the chivalrous thing. Shrugging, he sat across from her and folded his hands.

"You know that woman," he stated.

She nodded. "My ex is with her now. Actually, he was with her while he was still with me."

Chase winced. "That's why you didn't want to eat here. I'm sorry, Red."

Carrie waved a hand. "It's no biggie. I'm not still in love with him or anything."

"You were in love with him?"

She nodded. "We were living together, actually."

"That was a close call, then."

"What do you mean?"

"You almost spent your life with a guy who clearly didn't realize how good he had it."

That ridiculous statement made her smile. "I'll give you that."

Their lunches arrived, thankfully brought by one of the pool servers and not Brandi, and her hunger happily returned. Chase ordered a soda and she ordered a sparkling water. If she was going to do the caffeine-free thing, she wasn't going to settle for tap water.

"How's your day been going so far?" he asked her after a while.

"Good. Slow, but then Thursday mornings usually are. This afternoon and tomorrow will be a different story."

Chase nodded. "Yeah, I noticed how much more crowded the lobby was this morning even since yesterday."

Carrie nodded as she sipped at her bubbly water. "Business conferences. Vacationers. The weekends are usually wrapped up with weddings, but the prep for those guests is almost always taken care of during the week."

"The spa looks pretty busy. And I saw a lot of those soaps in your shop."

"Jo Potter's famous soaps, you mean."

"Yep. Billy and Shannon are trying their hand at the same type of business."

"I think they'll do really well."

"They're both into it with both feet. I'll give them that."

Carrie smiled as she recalled just how into it Shannon and her new husband really were. They were a unit, and she'd seen that almost from the beginning. Even before Shannon dipped her toes in the sand.

"Are you really going to work for Billy?"

A smile teased Chase's mouth. "He insists I'll be working with him, not for him."

"Billy can be pretty stubborn."

"Just how well did you get to know my cousin when he was down here?"

"I only know what I saw when he was pursuing Shannon. She was stubborn, too."

"They're perfectly matched, then."

She laughed lightly. "Definitely."

Chase pushed his now-empty plate aside and folded his hands on the table. "We Harris men can be very focused. We see what we want and, well, that's it."

"That's it?"

"Hey, my brother Zach is the word man. He can come up with some line of shit to calm the meanest bull any day. Billy and me? We're just doing our best."

His eyes were so intent. His face was a picture of confidence. It was very seductive, that kind of assuredness. She was sorely lacking in that department herself. She had to bring up her game for the little one that was coming. That was for sure.

Carrie reached across and touched his hand. It felt solid. Warm. "Your best is pretty darn good, Chase."

Chapter 6

Chase let Carrie's words wash over him. It was gratifying, because he was trying his damnedest to walk the razor-thin line between attentive and at-ease. This girl affected him like no other ever had, even if his own experience with the opposite sex was less than stellar.

"What are you doing Sunday?"

"Sunday?"

"Yeah. You're off, right?"

"Yes."

"Come out with me on Saturday night. You work a half-day, right? The girl at the spa desk said so."

"Thanks, Paula. Yes."

He let a smile curve his lips. "Then we'll spend Valentine's Day together."

Her pretty eyes went round. "Valentine's Day?"

"Sunday, Carrie." He quirked a brow. "Haven't you noticed all of the hearts strung just about everywhere?"

"They're hard to ignore."

"Then we'll spend it together."

She nibbled her lip, but then gave him a nod. "Okay."

"Don't worry, Red. I'll make it one you'll remember."

She leveled a look at him. "That's what I'm afraid of."

She sounded so serious he felt a tingle of unease. "What, exactly, are you afraid of?"

Carrie studied the top of the table for a long minute before facing him again. "I'm afraid that memories will be all I have."

Her statement was so sad his own heart sank. "That's not all, Carrie."

She started, and then nodded. "The baby."

He didn't grin, but he sure wanted to. "Yeah, the baby."

She shifted in her chair and he suspected she was going to say more about it. Set down some ground rules or something like that. Then her eyes shifted and she looked at a spot over his shoulder.

"Chase!" a woman called, causing him to turn and follow Carrie's gaze.

A woman raised a hand to him, her waist-length dark brown hair pulled back with a stretchy hairband like he'd noticed Carrie wore. From Billy's description of Jo Potter, he figured this had to be the woman herself.

"I'm so glad I caught you." Her eyes sparkled as she let out a breath. "Sorry to interrupt your lunch. Hi, Carrie."

"Hi, Jo," Carrie said with a smile.

"Chase Harris, Jo." Chase stood and held out a hand. "But I'm guessing you already figured that out."

Jo nodded. "Yep. I'm sorry Billy couldn't come down here but I'm very glad to meet you."

Chase dipped his head. "Likewise. Please, join us."

He held out one of the empty chairs at their table and Jo nodded and sat down.

"I'll be quick," she said. "I know we were supposed to meet later, but Ethan made some plans for this weekend that, apparently, start today!"

"For Valentine's Day," Chase guessed aloud, taking his seat once more.

Jo's smile was bright. "My husband loves to make grand gestures."

Billy had told Chase all about Jo's husband, billionaire Ethan Potter. He was one of the founders of the Serenity Shores Sand Dollars soccer club, and a driving force behind the proposed complex and tourist center. His wife's goat farm and petting zoo would be an unusual but very welcome addition to that plan.

"So," Jo went on. "We'll have to make arrangements to get the parcel to you next week sometime."

Chase nodded. "That works for me. Are you sure I can't just swing by and pick it up from one of your staff?"

Jo's brows shot up. "No way. Nobody touches Hamilton's stuff but me."

He blinked. "Hamilton?"

"My buck. Nasty little guy, but I love him." Jo laughed. "I'm pretty sure I'm the only one who does."

Chase looked at Carrie, who's eyes were sparkling. Just what did she know about this?

"Jo, what, exactly, am I taking back to Billy?" he asked.

"Hamilton's sperm, Chase."

Chase's mouth dropped open. "That's what I'm here for?"

Jo nodded. "I'll have it collected right before you head back to Cypress Corners. Then it will be frozen and readied for transport."

"Ready for transport," he repeated.

"Billy really didn't tell you?"

"He just said you wouldn't want to mail the package when I suggested that."

Jo laughed and Carrie grinned as he looked over at her.

"No," Jo said. "No, I wouldn't."

Chase sat back. "Goat sperm."

"Premium goat sperm, I'll have you know."

"Why wouldn't Billy just get a male goat himself?"

"A buck, you mean. And they can be very temperamental. He wants to open a petting zoo, right?"

"Yeah."

"Then there you go."

"There I go."

Jo patted his hand. "Don't worry. I'll call or text you when I'm back in Serenity Shores." She stood. "Carrie, always nice to see you."

"Nice to see you too, Jo."

Jo waved a hand as she crossed the restaurant towards the lobby. Chase was still processing when he caught Carrie's chuckle.

"What's so funny?" he asked, finding a smile.

"You should have seen your face."

"I was surprised, is all."

"Ha! You were shocked. Billy didn't tell you anything about just what you were doing down here?"

Chase shook his head. "Now I know why." He blew out a breath. "I have to feel a little sorry for old Hamilton, though."

"Why?"

"He misses out on all the fun."

That got him another laugh from her, and he grinned. Their baby had been made the old fashioned way, not that he'd known it at the time. Still, he felt his connection to Carrie grow as they shared the last of their meal before he took her back to the spa shop to finish out her day.

On Valentine's Day, though? He'd take a page from Ethan Potter's book and plan some kind of grand gesture to make her see that they could really make this thing work.

***

On Saturday evening Carrie ran a brush through her hair after she'd dressed for her date with Chase. She'd chosen to wear a pretty red cardigan over a creamy winter-white camisole, and paired the set with a slim dark brown leather skirt. It was Valentine's Day Eve, if that was such a thing.

Running her hands over her hips, she wondered at the life growing inside of her. By the time the weather turned warmer, and that would be sooner rather than later here on Crescent Key, she wouldn't be able to do up the back zipper of her skirt.

Thin cream tights and high leather books a shade darker than her skirt finished her outfit. She put on a little bit of makeup now, too. Mascara and a rosy lip gloss, along with a sweep of blush. She did nothing to hide her freckles. Doug had made fun of them, in a tone that had been just this side of disparaging. Jeez, how had she missed what a slug he was?

This was her second date—or was it her third?—with Chase, actually. Third dates had a certain aura around them. It was the next-step date. The next-base date. The take-it-up-a-notch date. Where, exactly, did that leave her?

She'd already been in the guy's bed. She'd been a willing and able participant in a stereotypical post-wedding hookup. Did the third-date rules apply in her particular situation?

A knock came at her door and she gave one last look in the bathroom mirror and turned out the light. Pulling the door open, she found Mrs. Battle standing there. A smile wreathed her rosy face, and her hands were folded over her perpetually-aproned middle.

"Hello, dear."

"Hi, Mrs. Battle. Did you need something?"

"Oh no, dear. I was just about to take a roasted chicken out of the oven and I wondered if you would like to join Mr. Battle and myself."

Carrie shook her head. "No, thank you."

Her brows furrowed above her round glasses. "But you often join us for dinner on Saturdays. Since Thanksgiving, anyway."

Don't I know it. "And I've enjoyed sharing your scrumptious meals, believe me. You and Mr. Battle have been very kind."

"Kind, shmind." Mrs. Battle's confusion turned to obvious interest as she ran her gaze over Carrie's outfit. "Look at you! Do you have a hot date?"

A flush washed over Carrie's cheeks. "I don't know about hot."

"Well, I do." Chase stepped behind Mrs. Battle, who gasped as she whirled to face him. "Good evening," he said to her.

Carrie ran her gaze over him. He was wearing pressed chinos and a thin sweater in a deep shade of green. It was a V-neck, and she could see just a glimpse of the crisp hair she knew were sprinkled over his finely-wrought chest. She mouthed his name, but very little sound pushed past her lips.

Her landlady giggled and twisted her apron in her hands. "Oh, aren't you a gentleman. Our Carrie could use a night out."

"Seriously?" Carrie squeaked.

"I'm Mary Battle," Mrs. Battle said. "And you are?"

Chase bowed his head. "Very nice to meet you, Mrs. Battle. I'm Chase Harris."

"Harris." Her mouth was an O as realization apparently struck her. "You're related to Shannon's Billy."

"I am indeed," he said with a smile.

Mrs. Battle stepped back to allow Chase to enter. "And you are our Carrie's hot date for the evening."

"Really?" Carrie was beginning to believe she was invisible, the way the two of them talked as if she wasn't standing there. "Hello, Chase."

"Hey there, Red," he said, at last turning those gorgeous hazel eyes in her direction. "Wow."

His one word of praise sent shivers through her. Mrs. Battle's eyes were twinkling and Carrie could just imagine the machinations beginning to spin in her mind. She'd told Carrie when she'd moved in that she'd felt thwarted that Shannon had managed to handle her love life without her careful intervention. Surely the woman wanted to meddle in Carrie's affairs now.

"Thank you again, Mrs. Battle," Carrie said with a smile. The woman was a dear, if meddlesome. "Maybe next Saturday?"

"Maybe next Saturday, what?" Chase asked.

"Dinner downstairs with Mr. Battle and myself, Chase." She brightened. "Oh, perhaps the both of you could join us?"

"I don't think Chase will still be in Serenity Shores next Saturday, Mrs. Battle."

Carrie heard Chase cough, or make some kind of sound like it. He was looking at her with a strange expression on his face. His eyes were dark and his lips in a thin line. She did a quick calculation and wondered if he just might still be around next weekend. But hadn't he said he was only here for a week?

"Or, maybe you will be?" she asked, trying to get on firmer footing.

A small shrug from him was her only answer.

"Oh, then at least promise me the two of you will think about dinner?" Mrs. Battle asked.

"We will," Carrie rushed out. "Thank you for the invitation."

Her landlady suddenly seemed to pick up on the murky undercurrent running between Carrie and Chase, and she fluttered her hands in a wave and hurried back downstairs.

"Sorry," Carrie said. "She's a little intrusive but very kind."

"Don't apologize. It's not your fault you don't know my plans."

"I guess that's true."

"For the record, I might not be around next weekend."

Carrie held onto the doorknob to do something. "When do you go back?"

"I'm not sure."

"Why not?"

Chase shook his head. "I'm at Crescent until Wednesday."

"But when do you go back, Chase?"

He leaned against the doorjamb. "That's entirely up to you, Red."

Alarm trilled through her. "I think you're giving me way too much power."

"Seems to me you never had much before now." He pushed off the jamb and took her hand in his. "Don't you think you deserve it?"

"Why?" she asked on a breath.

He smiled and heat washed over her. "You already have it over me, Carrie. You and that baby you're carrying."

Her heart dipped a little. This was because she was pregnant. Yes, he probably wanted to hook up again. Even she recognized that the night they'd shared had been incredible. But the reason he was making this full-court press? It had to be the baby he'd never had with his ex-wife.

"You look gorgeous, by the way," he added, bringing his lips to hers for a hot sweet kiss. "Are you ready to go?"

"Sure."

"Then let's hit it."

She grabbed her bag and locked up before following him down the staircase that clung to the back of the wood-framed house. She would focus on having a nice night out with a great guy. As for having any sort of power over him? She had every reason to believe it was all because of her little tagalong.

Why else would a guy like him want any kind of future with her?

Chapter 7

Chase wondered at the doubtful expression on Carrie's beautiful face. First there was the brush-off regarding dinner with her landlady. And then there was the complete lack of confidence. Didn't she know how hot she was? How sweet and funny? As strange as it might seem, the more time he spent with her the more time he wanted to spend with her. He'd actually missed seeing her the last couple of days.

He'd given her some space, hoping she would think a little bit about him and how they would spend the weekend together. And they would spend it together. He wanted to be with her because of her, and not just because she was having his baby.

He didn't know how to tell her that, though. He'd fucked up with Cheyanne after forcing a marriage on her. He wouldn't do that with Carrie.

His truck was parked in front of her place, and he held open the passenger door for her.

"Thank you." She climbed in and he took a second to admire her legs. They were long and strong, and he remembered just what they'd felt like against him. Around him.

"So what do you have planned for us tonight, Chase?"

He wriggled his eyebrows, winning a laugh from her. "Dinner, Red. And dessert."

"Okay. And after?"

"After? Hmm. I think we can probably come up with something."

She quirked a sideways glance at him but he just shook his head at her and walked around to his side of the truck. Turning the vehicle back towards the resort, he steered through the scant traffic. Saturday night must not be exactly hopping in the sleepy little town, but that was probably because most of the activity was centered in and around the resort.

He found out from the concierge that there was a big Valentine's Day party tomorrow evening, and wondered why Carrie hadn't mentioned it. She was just coming off of a bad breakup, or had been when she'd stumbled into his field of vision at Billy's wedding. The fact that the other woman was someone she could run into on any given day at Crescent had to add to her dislike of the lovers' holiday. It had never been one of his favorites. That was, until this year at least. Until spending it with Carrie had become a very real possibility.

"You didn't make a reservation at Wisteria, did you?" she asked, her voice small.

"No. Should I have?"

She gave a shake of her head and ran her fingers through that silky hair of hers. "No. I just didn't want you to make a fuss."

"Hey, whose Saturday night is this?"

She wrinkled her nose at him. "Yours, I guess?"

"Ours, Red. But I don't want to spend any of it at some stuffy restaurant."

"It's not stuffy, actually. Fantastic food and atmosphere, but not stuffy."

"Then we'll go there on our anniversary."

She gaped at him and he reached over to pat her leg. "I'm kidding, Carrie."

He'd managed to fill the past day and a half with the activities scheduled up and down the resort's beach. A lot of it was spent just staring out at the water, though. Trying to get a handle on what he wanted his future to be. He was pretty sure now, though. His future was sitting right next to him.

He had to rein it in a little bit. He was seized with the urge to push for more. To get a commitment from her that they could have an actual future. She so wasn't ready for any of it. Maybe after tonight she could give him a hint about the reason why.

He parked at the resort and turned to her as he cut the engine. She was staring at him, her eyes wide and shiny, and he leaned in for another kiss. The one they'd shared up in her funky old-fashioned apartment had been way too brief in his opinion. In hers too, unless he missed his guess. Her gaze had gone soft and a little hungry. Now she returned his kiss, cupping the side of his face with one hand.

"What are you up to, Chase?" she whispered, her mouth still close to his.

"Dinner." He brushed another kiss on her lips. "In my room."

She pulled back, her brows raised. "I've never been in the guest rooms!"

"I figured as much. And as sweet as your quirky little apartment is, I bet you could use some luxury."

"Luxury and power, Chase Harris? Sounds like a recipe for a romantic suspense novel."

"I have no clue what you're talking about, so I'll have to take your word on that." He got out and opened her door. He liked doing the little gentlemanly things for her. "Dinner should be here in about a half an hour."

"And what are you plans before?"

"I thought we could have a drink in the lounge." She arched a brow and he smiled. "Yours could be virgin, of course." He winced as she laughed at him. "Okay, my bad. That ship has sailed."

She grabbed on to his arm as they made their way into the lobby, the smile on her face bright. "You're a funny guy, you know that?"

"I never have been, but I'll take your word on that too."

The lounge was located just off the lobby, not far from the coffee shop. It was dimly-lit, but decorated with more paper hearts and strings of twinkle lights. It felt a little bit like being inside a greeting card, but he could deal with it. Carrie, with her red hair and soft red sweater fit right into the scenery.

They found a table near the huge fireplace, a small round thing with two chairs. He held her chair for her, an act which she always seemed to find humorous, and then sat across from her.

"So, virgin huh?" she teased, picking up the small cardboard sign in the center of the table. "I bet one of these chocolate martinis would be great, but then it would just be chocolate milk."

"In a fancy glass." He held up a hand to signal one of the servers. "I say you get it with extra chocolate sauce."

She stared at him for a second, and then caught his meaning. He'd been teasing about extra chocolate sauce the other night in

Rancho Casa. Her cheeks flushed a pretty pink and she gave an enthusiastic nod.

Suddenly, the prospect of rekindling the heat from their first night together felt like a distinct possibility.

***

Carrie arched upward towards Chase, craving more of his touch. Drinks had been fun and relaxed. Their room-service dinner had been remarkable. But this? Letting him slowly undress her in front of the flames flickering behind the glass fireplace screen surpassed anything she could have imagined might happen tonight.

The plush carpet beneath her was thick and soft, and the lighting in the room was low. He'd cracked the doors to the balcony, and she could just hear the lapping of the waves on the shore below. Apparently he adhered to the third-date rule as well, and was rapidly sending any thoughts of even a token refusal far from her mind.

"Christ, you're beautiful," he breathed, nuzzling the side of her neck as his hands trailed over her breasts. "I thought I might have been remembering that night through beer goggles, but damn."

She ran her fingers through his thick hair. It was silky and cool beneath her fingers, at odds with the rough edge of his tongue hot on her skin between her breasts. "This feels so good, Chase."

The pregnancy must be making her breasts extra-sensitive, because every lick and pinch sent heat sparking through her body. He was teasing her nipples now, first one and then the other, until her pulse pounded. She was wearing nothing but a lacy pink bra and panties, her sweater and skirt were somewhere over by the door along with her boots, but by the appreciation clear in his eyes he found her as arousing as she found him. And he was. He was wearing far too many clothes, though.

She placed a hand in the middle of his chest and pushed at him. He lifted his head to face her, a lazy grin on his face. "What is it, baby?"

Leaning up on her elbows, she ran her eyes over him. "You have to catch up, Chase."

His smile widened. "I told you I was a gentleman." He sat back, winking as he pulled his thin sweater up and over his head. His gaze fell down to his pants as he unbuttoned and began to unzip.

His chest as even better than she'd remembered, every sculpted dip and ridge catching the low light to make her shiver.

She'd been with him already. In several different ways that night over a month and a half ago. She wanted to feel that chest tight against her, the light dusting of crisp hairs tickling and teasing her breasts.

Then he stood and dropped his pants and her mouth went dry. The black boxer briefs hugged his erection, reminding her of just how perfectly he'd fit her. There were sexy dents on either side of his narrow hips, and she couldn't help but come up on her knees and grab onto his butt as she kissed the middle of his chest.

"Ah, Red." His fingers ran through her hair now, slow and deep as he sank down to his knees. He brought her face up to his. "I'm going to make you feel so good."

She ran her hands over his chest now, unable to keep from letting out a purr. "You feel so good, Chase."

She was on her back again, and her pulled aside the cups of her bra to suckle her. His hand was between her legs, urging her thighs apart as he stroked her. She was so tightly wound now, every stroke sending her higher. Dragging his mouth from one breast to another, he growled and kissed his way down to join his clever fingers.

"Chase!" She gasped as his teeth grazed her through her panties. "Oh!"

And then his mouth was fixed to her flesh, his tongue delving inside as he cupped her butt in both his hands. She couldn't grab on to a thought as he focused every bit of attention on that tiny, hungry part of her. Trembling, she surrendered as her climax came roaring over her. Her limbs tensed and then sank into the carpet.

Chase was braced above her, a look of masculine pride on his face. "Damn, I could watch you come all night."

She managed to pull in a breath and let it out with a sigh. "I don't think I'd survive."

He stood, holding a hand out to her. "Let's get on the bed, Carrie. If you can't walk tomorrow, I don't want it to be due to laying on the floor."

She took his hand and let him pull her to her feet. Her legs were still shaking, and she leaned against his strong frame. "Just what should it be due to, then?"

He draped his arms around her, holding her tight. "Purely to my loving, baby."

His erection was hot and hard against her belly and she stifled another shiver. "I'm not sure if this is a good idea."

"It's a great idea, Red. We have this, this, heat between us. From the start. Can you deny it?"

"Not at all. But we still don't know that much about each other."

His brow furrowed but his hands began stroke her back. "We have a lot to discuss, Carrie. I hear you. And we will."

"But not tonight?" She held onto his shoulders and came up on her toes. "Is that what you're saying?"

"If that's okay with you."

She thought for a long minute. He made her feel so good. It had been too long before that first time together. She'd half-believed it had been due to her romance drought after Doug and the abundance of alcohol at the wedding, but tonight disabused her of that idea. Chase was an expert at knowing just how to make her forget everything but how good they could make each other feel.

Dropping back down to her knees, she caressed him through the thin fabric of his briefs. He groaned, tunneling his fingers through her hair again. He cupped the back of her head, but not in a way that made her feel trapped. No, his intensity fueled her libido and urged her without words to please him.

He was hot and huge in her hands as she pushed the waistband of his briefs down below his groin. She had never been very comfortable pleasing a man this way, but she just let her instincts take over as she proceeded to drive him as crazy as he'd just made her.

"Damn, Red." He made that sexy growl again and bucked a little. "Damn."

It didn't take long to bring him to the brink. Teasing him for a while longer just because she could, she finally took him completely in her mouth and showed him some mercy. He never lost his rigid stance, even as he shuddered in his release.

"Carrie, baby," he rasped.

She came to her feet and kissed his open mouth. "Yes?"

"Stay here with me tonight?"

Her mind spun as she tried to think of a reason she shouldn't stay with him at the resort. There was no one to really worry about her tonight. Even Mrs. Battle wouldn't take much note of Carrie's absence. She didn't have to work tomorrow, which was another point to consider.

"I don't know," she said, her conviction sounding weak to her own ears.

"Please, baby?"

She heard a tenderness in his voice, but that had to be a result of the stellar orgasm she'd just given him. He looked so sweet, though. As sweet as any guy as hot as he could look nearly naked, that was.

Biting her lip, she nodded.

His smile was slow, but lit his eyes with golden fire.

"Then let's take this to bed."

Chapter 8

Chase stretched his arms, the wide bed comfortable beneath him. Carrie was curled against his side, her body as naked as his. He'd never spent the night with a woman since his divorce, and never this close and cozy. Cheyanne wasn't one for tenderness, but he never blamed her. He had no clue how to reach across the acres of bedding that seemed to be between them after the first few months of their marriage.

The thin curtains at the windows opposite the bed framed the sky beyond. It was getting lighter outside, the morning of Valentine's Day dawning. He had a bundle of contented woman in his arms, the mother of his baby, and he wasn't sure how he felt about it. Last night had been amazing, from the love play in front of the fire to holding her close all night.

She stirred and he stared down at her as her eyes fluttered open. "I'm sorry I conked out on you last night."

He shrugged. "I figured it had something to do with the pregnancy, Red. So I'm all kinds of ready to give you the benefit of the doubt."

She smiled up at him, brushing a few thick curls off her forehead. "You are a gentleman." She laughed softly. "That's a sentence I never thought I'd say while naked and tangled up with a guy."

He gave her a one-armed hug. "I can't say another round wouldn't have been fantastic, but I didn't go to bed wanting."

Amazingly, she blushed. It must be something with redheads, because it seemed like every emotion was clear on her lightly-freckled cheeks. Unable to resist, he turned and brought his mouth to hers. Just as he was about to kiss her, a knock sounded at the door. Grunting, he sat up and pushed his hair back from his brow.

"I ordered breakfast," he told her.

She ran her gaze over his chest and down to where the sheets just covered his dick. "When?"

"Last night."

Her head tilted. "Before you asked me to stay over?"

"Hey, a guy can hope."

She didn't seem too put out by his assumptions, so he threw back the sheets and got out of the bed to walk across the room to grab his pants off of the floor. "Just a minute," he called towards the door.

Buttoned and zipped, he pulled on his rumpled sweater and opened the door to let in the kid with the meal cart. He'd never been a romance-and-roses kind of guy, but he was glad that the resort had thought of those romantic touches this morning. He tipped the kid, closed the door and checked out the cart.

A simple meal of scrambled eggs, fruit, juice and coffee was elevated by the same fine china and silverware he'd noticed at last night's dinner. Tiny hearts cut out of glossy paper were sprinkled across the snowy-white tablecloth and a handful of red roses stood in a clear crystal vase in the center of the rolling table.

"That looks lovely."

He looked up to find Carrie wrapped in a sheet. It draped off one shoulder and her hair was swept to cover the bare skin he saw. She looked like some kind of goddess, all rosy and sweet.

"They do a pretty good breakfast. I hope you eat eggs."

"I do."

He poured himself a coffee and pointed to a box of teabags. "I asked for some decaf options."

Her brows raised. "That's very thoughtful."

She sat down on the padded ottoman next to the table, so he settled on the couch across from her.

"You know, I didn't think to ask," he said. "Are you sick in the morning?"

She held a piece of toast just shy of her mouth and shook her head. "Not very often. Not yet, anyway."

"Well, what I know about pregnancy comes from TV shows," he said.

"Me, too." He raised his brows and she shrugged. "Only child, remember?"

He nodded. "I'd like to come with you when you go to the doctor."

Alarm sparked in her eyes. "I hadn't thought about that, but I guess that would be okay."

He set his coffee cup down and reached across to cover her hand with his. "Carrie, I'm not pushing. I swear. This is all new for me."

She nodded. "For me, too."

The mood had turned decidedly deflated in a hot minute, so he served them from the platter of eggs and bacon and dug in himself. She ate, he was happy to see.

"So what should we do on our first Valentine's Day?" he asked.

She stared at him for a beat. "Our first?"

He spread his hands in an effort to block the frustration he was feeling. "Look, I know we're not getting married but we will be in each other's lives."

"I know." Her voice was small and he felt like a complete jerk for pushing her. "What would you like to do?"

He brightened. "How about taking one of the cruises they offer down at the dock? It'll be a little bit chilly but not too bad."

She seemed to consider his idea. "I've never done that. Been on one of those cruises, that is."

"Then I'll make the arrangements." He winked at her sheet-clad body. "As much as I like seeing you nearly naked, you might want to rethink your wardrobe."

She laughed at that, and the weirdness between them seemed to dissipate completely. "Okay. Can you drop me home so I can change?"

He nodded. "Sure thing. You might want to grab a couple of things for later, too."

"Are you asking me to stay over again, Chase? You know I'm working tomorrow."

The sparkle in her eyes told him she wouldn't mind if he did. He sure as hell wanted to roll around with her in that big bed again, this time closing the deal. Not that all of the petting, and the best blowjob he'd ever gotten, hadn't been eye-opening. He just wanted to be inside her again. If his memory of their first time together was any indication, they were perfectly suited in that aspect too.

"I'll leave the staying-over decision completely up to you, Red."

She beamed a smile. "Putting me in the driver's seat, are you?"

Naughty images flashed through his mind, fueled by one particular recollection of her taking control during their first night together. He didn't even try to hide the desire her words sent flashing over him.

"Hey, if the lady wants to drive who am I to argue?"

***

Carrie sat in Wisteria, still amazed that Chase had been able to pull this off. She had no idea how he'd managed to reserve a table for them. The very popular, very well-reviewed restaurant was someplace she never thought she would frequent. The prices alone put it outside her salesgirl salary.

She felt her dress fit in, at least. Buying off season, not that Serenity Shores really had an off season, gave her the opportunity to build her wardrobe. Just a few dressy pieces for the times Doug had business dinners with clients.

He'd always wanted her to look just right, which should have been yet another clue that he wasn't the guy for her forever. Still, the scooped-neck jersey clung in all the right places. She idly realized it was a good thing the weather would be turning warm again soon, since she wouldn't fit into it again until next winter.

The dinner had been intimate despite the crowded dining area. The food had been phenomenal, though to be fair it wasn't every day that she dined on a simple yet amazing lobster dish she couldn't name and a nearly-rare filet that seemed to satisfy the little carnivore she was apparently carrying.

Chase had called the concierge to book their cruise before taking her back to her place to change that morning. Mrs. Battle hadn't tried to hide as she watched them through her front window, her eyes bright and her smile wide. It the lady wasn't such a dear, Carrie would have told her to mind her own business. It was kind of nice having someone look out for her, but that didn't necessarily mean that she wanted to be watched like a teenager on a first date.

The cruise had been a little bit fun and a whole lot romantic. She was falling for this guy in spite of her best intentions, and she was swiftly running out of reasons to keep him at arms' length. Figuratively, at least. She hadn't thought to refuse getting naked with him last night for more than a hot minute.

"So, how am I doing?" he asked her.

"Doing what, exactly?"

"Pouring on the romance, Red." He leaned back, looking very yummy in his thin gray cable sweater. "It's what the day's for, isn't it?"

Since she'd never had a serious boyfriend for the holiday, she would just have to take his word for it. "Sure."

He blinked at her. "Are you feeling okay?"

Plastering on a smile, she nodded. "Just a little tired, I guess."

He sprang out of his seat like his butt was on fire. "Let me get the check."

Before she could stop him, he was taking long purposeful steps towards the servers' station to find their waiter. Carrie sat back and sipped at her sparkling cider. Served in a crystal flute, she figured that anybody watching her would think she was sipping champagne. She so wasn't ready to out her little bundle, and since Shannon left she didn't really have anybody she was close to. Marion was darn near perfect, but she was still her boss. Carrie's inner circle was pretty empty, actually.

Shannon was up in Cypress Corners. Mrs. Battle, as sweet as she was, wasn't exactly a tell-all-your-secrets-to kind of lady. So that left Paula, who she was only just getting to know.

Chase came back, worry clear in his hazel eyes. "The bill's all set, Carrie." He stepped behind her chair, pulling it back as she stood. "Let's get out of here."

A thrill went through her as his fingers brushed over her nape. She was discovering that Chase was very demonstrative, and she had never been one for public displays. His every touch wasn't too much or possessive, though. No, he somehow managed to put a tenderness into even the simplest brush of his fingertips. It was probably what made him the best lover she'd ever had, not that the pool was extensive.

"Are we headed to your room?" she asked on a breath.

Heat flared in his gaze. "Damn, I sure hope so."

His words were simple and honest, yet a pull of desire tightened her core. There was something here, something she didn't dare name as love. She would enjoy him while he was here and, hopefully, see what they could be to each other going forward with their mutual responsibility.

Back in his room, he pulled her close. "I love the way you feel in my arms, Red."

She ran her hands over his chest, letting herself lean against him. "Your arms feel pretty great around me, Chase."

He brought that amazing mouth of his to hers and just rubbed gently against her lips. It was ticklish and hot, and made her itch for more. Coming up on her toes, she pressed her tongue against his parted lips and drove inside. He groaned, and his grip on her tightened. They had this, then. Instant and complete sexual attraction.

It had led them to this situation. That was for sure. But would it be enough to help them form any kind of future? She knew she wanted him. In her bed and in her space. He was fun and charming as all get out. Hot and handsome and an incredible lover. He wanted to be a part of their baby's life, too. She might not know much about this particular set of circumstances, but Chase's brand of "hot dad" was something to consider.

"Come to bed, baby," he rasped, his lips on the side of her neck. His tongue darted over her pulse and she shivered. "Come to bed and I'll let you drive."

Desire coiled tighter still.

"Oh, yes," she breathed.

His big hands grabbed her butt and he walked her over to the bed. Setting her down gently, he stepped back and started to get naked. Ooh, she could watch him all night but there was a certain amount of driving she so wanted to experience.

99

She kicked off her shoes and came up on her knees, shedding her dress. He paused, his thumbs dragging his pants down low. She eyed that strip of lighter skin, well below his navel, with that thin strip of dark brown hair.

"You're really beautiful, do you know that?" he asked, his voice low.

She'd never been called that before. Pretty, maybe. Cute, most definitely. Doug had been very effusive in his compliments but they were usually on what she was wearing or how her hair was done. Usually as either related to complimenting his own fine full-of-himself self.

"Chase." Her voice was low too, and if he was paying as close attention to it as he clearly was to her breasts, he would hear how much she wanted him. "Come to bed."

He stripped and her bra and panties were gone in the next minute. His hands were everywhere, and hers weren't playing shy either. He let her drive, just as he'd promised, and having him beneath her was so arousing that she was nearly crying with relief as she finally took him high up inside of her.

He wore protection, but even as she admired his ability to think of it she figured that horse was already out of the barn. His big body strained beneath her, his hard belly stroking her just right as she rode him.

Sweet, naughty words filled her ears as she bowed back, letting his hands run all over the front of her. Her thighs trembled as she squeezed tighter still, making him groan as she neared her release.

And when she climaxed, clutching at his wrists as he held on to her hips, she screamed his name.

"Ah, Red." He shuddered beneath her as he joined her in release. "Damn…"

Still breathing fast, she collapsed against his chest, her legs useless as they draped on either side of him. His hands were gentle on her back, his fingers tunneling through her hair again.

"I love you," he breathed in her ear.

She froze. *Oh, God.* Time and time again, Doug had said that to her. After they would make love, it was the first thing out of his mouth.

"Um," she stammered. "I have to go."

She managed to climb off of him with very little grace, ignoring him as he sat up and brushed his hair back from his face.

"Where are you going?"

She grabbed her bra and panties, holding them in front of her despite the fact that they gave her very little protection.

"I have to work tomorrow," she said stupidly. "I have to go home."

"Well, give me a second and I'll take you."

"No, no. That's okay."

As she backed up she stumbled over her shoes on the plush carpet. Her shoes! She wouldn't think about the implications. She'd kicked them off, sure. But that didn't mean she was in love with Chase. She couldn't be.

"Carrie, I'll drive you home." He stood, gloriously naked and clearly confused.

She really had no choice at the moment. She gave him a small nod of agreement.

They both dressed in silence, and the drive to her place was just as awkward as that reverse strip-tease. He drew her to him to kiss her good night, but she turned her head to just brush his cheek with her lips.

"Good night, Chase."

And then she was out of there. Every step up that narrow staircase to her apartment, every beat of her racing heart, made her certain she was doing the right thing.

She was darned if she would make another mistake. Not when she had more to consider than her own feelings.

Chapter 9

"What the hell just happened?" Chase murmured.

He watched her house long after she'd disappeared around the back of it, trying to figure out just how he'd fucked up. They'd been having a great time, brushing over all the romantic stuff tied up with Valentine's Day as they'd shared some fun and food. The cruise had been tame but he'd enjoyed it, mainly because she was there beside him. What was it about this girl? From the jump, he'd only been able to see her. Once he'd caught sight of her at the wedding, she'd been the only one on his mind.

"And yet, you let her go back home to Serenity Shores without so much as a text." He put the truck in gear and drove back towards the resort. "Jackass."

She was carrying his baby, though. That seemed to draw him even closer to her. She turned him on like no other woman ever had, and it seemed like she enjoyed everything he did to her rosy little body. Just as he'd let her take the reins in his bed not even a half hour ago, he'd marveled that they were so perfectly matched. He'd come so hard he'd nearly passed out, and he had briefly wondered if his guest room was soundproof as she screamed in pleasure.

After, though. Holding her in his arms as they both cooled their jets. That had been amazing. The truth struck him like kick in the ass from one of Wild Harry's prize bulls.

He'd told her he loved her. What the fuck? No wonder she'd wanted to get the hell out of there, and fast. He was pushing for too much too soon, just like he had with Cheyanne.

"Look how great that turned out," he muttered. "Shit."

Once back in his guest room, he grabbed a bottle of beer out of the mini-fridge and sat himself out on the balcony. He took a long draw on his beer and settle back.

It was dark now, the moon low and fat over the gulf. It was a perfect night for lovers, not that he and Carrie had ever been that. A hookup, sure. And a repeat performance that eclipsed what they'd shared before, at least from where he was sitting. And where was he sitting now? Alone, that was where.

His phone dinged in his pocket, and for a second he thought she might be texting him. Drawing it out, he saw that he had a message from Billy.

Just touching base. Call me tomorrow?"

Instead of texting back, Chase tapped on the name and made a call.

"Chase, I didn't expect you to call me back," Billy said.

"I had the time, cuz. What's up?"

Billy was quiet for a long minute. "What's up with you? You sound terrible."

Chase laughed without humor. "I fucked up, that's what's up with me."

Billy let out a whistle. "What did you do, man?"

Chase took another sip of his beer. "I started up with Carrie again, Billy. And it was as good as it was at your wedding."

"So…why do you sound like you slipped in cow shit?"

Chase found a genuine laugh at his cousin's words. "She's pregnant, Billy. First, I asked her to marry me and tonight I told her I loved her."

"You what? Are you out of your mind?"

"Yeah, I shouldn't have suggested we get married."

"You suggested? What the hell is wrong with you?"

"Okay, that was the first day. Tonight I made things a whole lot worse."

"You've been down there less than a week. How bad could it be?"

"I told Carrie I loved her, Billy. Did you miss that part?"

"Okay, I heard that. Do you?"

106

"I don't know. She had just…we had just…and I guess my mouth got away from my brain."

"It's Valentine's Day, cuz. Are you serious?"

"I wasn't thinking."

Billy started to say something but Shannon's voice came on the line. "What did you do, Chase?"

Now Chase could count the conversations he'd had with Billy's wife on one hand. Tonight, though? Maybe he could use a little feminine perspective.

"Carrie's pregnant."

Stunned silence met his ears, swiftly followed by a high-pitched squeal of some words he couldn't quite make out. Shannon was laughing and sighing and making all sorts of crazy sounds.

"Chase, that's amazing!"

He'd held the phone away as she'd exploded but brought it close again. "I don't know how amazing it is. I was surprised, but I want us to be a family."

"Ooh, that's so sweet!" she said.

"I guess. She wasn't ready for that idea, though. And then, tonight, I told her I love her."

"Wait, what? Do you know what happened with her ex?"

"I know he cheated on her. He was a dickhead. What does that have to do with me."

"Chase, he told her all the time that he loved her. He was always making these grand gestures and acting like the most romantic boyfriend in the world."

Chase sat up, clutching his beer bottle tight. "Christ, you're kidding me."

"I'm not. When he hurt her, it completely blindsided her."

"No wonder she ran out of here like her hair was on fire."

"Ran out of there? Where are you...? Never mind. You're in the big beautiful Crescent guest room Billy booked."

"Yep. Why, are you wishing you had come down here with him after all?"

"Not even a little bit. I'm happy right here."

Chase felt a twinge of envy. That was what he wanted for himself. With Carrie. With their baby.

"Do you think I can make this right?"

"I think you have to. Here. Let me give you to Billy. He convinced me to put my toes in the sand."

"What the hell does that mean?"

She sighed loudly over the phone. "Serenity Shores, Chase. Toes in the sand, heart in your hand. Duh. It's only one of their most famous slogans."

"Toes?"

"Jeez, you're dense."

The line crackled a little and Billy came back on.

"What are you going to do?"

"I have one job here, cuz. Get that sample from Jo Potter, thanks for telling me what it was by the way, and get back to Cypress Corners."

"That's your one job?"

"Look, I fucked up my marriage by pushing for something that wasn't there. I don't want to do that with Carrie."

"There's a baby, man. How do you feel about that?"

Warmth spread through Chase, from his belly and up to his heart. "I feel like I'm the luckiest guy in the world. Carrie's a great girl, and I know our kid will be lucky to have her."

He heard Shannon sob and Billy chuckled. "I have you on speaker, man. So what about you?"

"What about me?"

"Would you be lucky to have her?"

Chase considered Billy's question for a hot minute before the truth struck him. "Yeah. I love her."

"Then you know what you have to do, don't you?"

"Not even a little bit." Chase grunted. "I want to make this right."

"Then figure out how to show her you're not just saying what you think she wants to hear. Proposing too fast. Saying you love her."

"But I *do* love her."

Again, Shannon's happy little squeal came over the line and he refrained from holding the phone away from his ear again.

"You can fix this," Billy said. "You fixed our relationship, didn't you?"

"I did?"

"We're talking about real things, man. Did we ever do that before?"

A smile curved Chase's lips. "Nah. Feels good."

"Yeah," Billy said. "It does."

Silence stretched between them and Chase marveled at the connection he had with Billy now.

"Okay, that's enough bro-mance for now," Shannon put in. "Go to her, Chase. Tell her what you told us."

Chase snorted. "Just like that?"

"Carrie is a levelheaded girl," Shannon said. "She wants to be happy, like anybody else. Can you make her happy?"

"I think so."

She clicked her tongue. "Nope. Not good enough."

"Okay then, yes. I can make her happy."

"Then my job here is done! Now your cousin and I have to get back to our Valentine's Day, if you don't mind."

Chase chuckled. "Okay, okay. I'll see you two next week."

"Let me know what happens, Chase," Shannon said. "If you don't, I'm going to call Carrie myself."

With that, Billy and his wife disconnected the call. Shannon was right, of course. Chase had to step it up. He wanted Carrie to be happy. Carrie wanted to be happy, too.

He just had to figure out how to make her see that he was the one guy who could make her happy for the rest of her life.

***

By Tuesday morning, Carrie couldn't ignore the truth. This wasn't about lines on a plastic stick, though. That particular fact remained unchanged. Nausea had met her yesterday morning and this morning, so it was clear her little rancher baby was holding on.

111

When she thought about her coming child, she was seized with such protectiveness it nearly stole her breath. This blessing had come out of nowhere yet she wanted to give her baby the best possible future. Why, then, had she run away from its father?

The truth was, his declaration had terrified her. Not that a man like him loved her, or thought he did. She couldn't imagine a better man to have a child with. To spend a life with. What scared her was that she had wanted to tell him she loved him too. And how silly was that?

Now it was late afternoon and here was another truth she couldn't ignore. She'd waited for the past two days for him to call her, even as she was dreading what she would have to say to him. Would he repeat his declaration? Did she want him to?

"What's with the long face?" Marion said as she stepped into the spa shop.

Carrie looked up from the register to face her boss. "Long face?"

"Sorry. It was the end of an old joke. You know, then the pig says to the horse?" She laughed and waved a hand. "Never mind. I thought you'd like that, what with your cowboy guy and all."

"Chase is a rancher, not a cowboy."

Marion shrugged. "Potato, po-tah-to."

Carrie found a smile. "How's the spa doing today?"

"Paula has her hands full but she seems to be handling it."

"So do you finally forgive Shannon for defecting?" Carrie teased.

"Nothing to forgive. I saw how she and Billy were together. It was inevitable."

Carrie knew there was nothing to say to that. Tidying up the sales counter was a way to avoid the piercing look on Marion's face. Finally she faced her again.

"What?" she asked in a small voice.

"I thought I saw that with you and Chase, Carrie." Her tone was soft now. "Tell me I was wrong?"

Tears stung her eyes and her throat felt tight. "He told me he loves me."

Marion's eyes went round. "Oh, that's… Wait. You don't look too happy about that."

"You remember Doug the Slug, don't you?" Carrie sniffled. "He told me that all the time. Showered me with all sorts of so-called proof of his devotion. It was all a lie."

Marion nodded. "If it helps in any way, I heard that he and Brandi split. Seems he was continuing his disgusting pattern."

"Well, then I'm sorry for her." She meant that, too. She held no ill will towards Brandi. "At least she knew enough not to move in with him."

"So what are you going to do about Chase?"

"There's nothing to do. I haven't seen him since Sunday night, and he's probably already left Serenity Shores."

"No, he hasn't. Jo Potter told me he's heading out to her farm tomorrow morning."

Carrie nodded. "Then he's leaving tomorrow. Same, same."

Marion smiled at the customer browsing the soy candles and stepped closer. "Something's up, Carrie. You can tell me anything. Remember how we teamed up on Shannon last summer?"

"Teamed up or ganged up?" Carrie smiled. "No, I know."

"Then, spill."

Carrie sucked in a breath. "Marion, I'm pregnant."

Her boss looked stunned, her mouth agape and her brows high. "Pregnant?" she asked in a low voice.

"Yes." Carrie blew out a breath. "Oh, it feels good to let that secret out."

"I take it Chase knows? Um, it is his right?"

That made Carrie smile a little bit. "Yes. And yes, he does know."

Marion snapped her fingers. "That's why you're afraid."

"Afraid?" Carrie squared her shoulders. "Afraid of what?"

"He said he loves you and you ran screaming."

"Not screaming, but yes. What's your point?"

"Do you think he's lying?"

"No," Carrie answered quickly. "From what I know of Chase, he tells the truth."

"That's my impression, too. Almost to his own regret, according to what he's said about his childhood."

Carrie thought for a minute. His relationship with his brother and father, with Billy, was strained by his own admission. It made sense that his truthfulness could have been a dual-edged sword.

"Then he really loves me?"

"I don't think that's the real question, Carrie. Do you?"

Carrie nibbled her lower lip, her mind whirring. "I could love him, Marion. He's sweet and hot and the father of my baby."

"Then what are you going to do?"

"What can I do? We haven't even talked since he brought me home Sunday night."

"So you don't have his number?"

"I have his number. I just don't know what I would say."

Marion held up her hands. "Hey, that's all on you." Her eyes strayed to Carrie's midsection and then back to her face. "Don't you think you owe it to that little nugget of yours to figure it out and fast?"

"I do."

Marion came behind the counter and gave her a hug. Carrie squeezed her eyes shut, one tear leaking through her lashes. Collecting herself, she wiped at her eye and stepped back. A quick glance around the shop showed her they were alone at least. That was one small consolation.

"Let me know if I have to find another girl to run the shop?"

Carrie stared at her for a beat. "What?"

"If what I think is going to happen happens, you'll join Shannon up there in Cypress Corners."

"I don't know about that."

Marion patted her arm. "Honey, I do. You'll want to be where your heart is. Apparently it's wherever your cowboy, sorry rancher, is."

Marion returned to the spa and Carrie started her evening shut-down. As she let the routine soothe her, her mind worked. She did love Chase. He was outrageous and sweet, and so earnest she had to face the fact that he always meant what he said. He'd told her as much, hadn't he? Then why couldn't she give him the benefit of the doubt?

Leaving Serenity, she headed through the lobby with a new purpose. She was going to tell Chase that she loved him and that was that. Her stomach in knots, she paused outside his door. She could hear the low rumble of his voice, a rough laugh reached her. Oh, no. He wasn't alone?

Shoving aside the memory about Doug's betrayal, she rapped on the door anyway. The door swung open to reveal Chase, shirtless and holding his phone to his ear.

"Okay, man. I'll see you tomorrow afternoon." He ended the call and looked at her. "Red?"

"Chase, I love you." She winced. What the heck was wrong with her? "I mean, can we talk?"

A smile replaced the surprise on his face as he ushered her into the room. "You love me?"

"I do. I'm sorry to interrupt."

"What, this?" He held up his phone. "I was just telling Billy that I would be bringing Hamilton's sample back to Cypress tomorrow."

"Then, you're alone?"

He closed the door, the smile never leaving his face. "Who would I be with, Carrie? You're the only one I want."

Tears filled her eyes, and this time she didn't bother brushing them away. "I was silly to run off, Chase."

"And I was stupid to blurt out the truth like that."

"It is the truth." She was sure of that now. "You love me."

"I do."

"Then Marion was right."

"Marion, your boss?"

Carrie gave a nod. "She'll have to find somebody else to run the spa shop, Chase. I'm going to be up in Cypress with you."

He let out a whoop and grabbed her to him. "Red, I promise to never give you the chance to regret this."

"And I promise to give you the family you've always wanted."

His eyes sparkled. "You know me. Damn, you really know me."

"I love you."

He held her closer still, and she realized that her heart was right to give him this chance. To give him her heart.

He would keep it, and their baby safe forever.

Discover other books by JoMarie DeGioia

The Secret Hearts series, including

The Courtesan Countess

The Bridgewater Brides series, including

The Heir's Treasure

The Viscount's Vixen

The Earl's Beauty

The Gentlemen Undercover series, including

A Hero and a Gentleman

The Shopgirls of Bond Street series, including

That Determined Mister Latham

The Dashing Nobles series, including

More Than Passion

Pride and Fire

Just Perfect

More Than Charming

The Cloud Canyon series, including

Chasing Dreams

Secret Dreams

Wildest Dreams

The Cypress Corners series, including

Finding Harmony

Taming Jake

Loving Cassie

Winning Ben

Showing Jessie

Seeing Shannon

Dreaming Eli

Giving Chase

Kissing Bree

Wishing Joy

Bugging Nate

The Gifted YA Fantasy/Adventure Trilogy, including

Gifted

Braunachs of the Dell series, including

Luke's Gold

Patrick's Promise

Sexy Historical Novellas, including

In the Lady's Heart

In the Baron's Bed

In the Knight's Chamber

Connect with me online

Twitter: https://twitter.com/JoMarieDeGioia

Facebook:

https://www.facebook.com/JoMarie.DeGioia.Author

Website: www.jomariedegioia.com

About the Author

JoMarie DeGioia is a bestselling author of Historical and Contemporary Romance. She's known Mickey Mouse from the "inside," has been a copyeditor for her tiny town's newspaper, and a bookseller. She is the author of nearly 50 Romances, and writes Young Adult Fantasy/Adventure stories and Paranormal Romance too. She gets lost in DIY projects around the house and works out plot ideas during long runs. She divides her time between Central Florida and New England.